PORTRAIT OF HIS OBSESSION

ANNIVERSARY EDITION

MICHELLE M. PILLOW

MICHELLEPILLOW.COM

*He knew for certain that she belonged forever in his arms,
just as he knew she didn't realize it yet."
– Portrait of His Obsession*

Not all obsessions are bad.

Lord Harrison, Earl of Wrotham, once lived from pleasure to pleasure—until the night he set eyes on his best friend's sister. Surely the beautiful temptress who danced under the moonlight couldn't be the same prim and proper lady of rumor. Instantly smitten, he sets out to tame his roguish ways, molding himself into the kind of man he is sure will please her. Only then will he get close enough to discover if she has a wild soul like his own, waiting to be released from the constraints of society.

Knowing the earl's reputation as a scoundrel, Elizabeth Blakeney has no choice but to ignore the man's advances...until her artist brother reveals an unflattering picture he has painted of her. It seems only the seductive earl can see beyond the likeness to the woman she longs to be. Should she rebel against society and the damning portrait, throwing caution to the wind? Or should she remain as she appears, as reserved and unfeeling as paint on canvas?

To my readers

Join the Reader Club Mailing List to stay informed about new books, sales, contests and preorders!

michellepillow.com/author-updates

CALDWELL COUNTRY ESTATE, NORTH OF
LONDON, ENGLAND, SPRING 1868

"Please, Thomas, do hurry. My arms grow weary of this pose. I have no wish to see my portrait painted in such a way. Why can't I sit on the swing?"

Elizabeth Blakeney sighed heavily, pretending to be more annoyed than she really was. She loved her brother dearly. He was her only family and her guardian—not to mention the Viscount Caldwell.

The morning was warm, filled with the floral scent of a refreshing country breeze. Thomas had posed her in the garden, near a broken stone wall. Roses climbed with small, orderly beauty. He refused to have the wall mended, saying that nature and time had perfected that which he could only hope to duplicate with paint and brush.

However, the wall was the only thing in disrepair at Caldwell Manor. The country estate was a beautiful haven, away from London where Thomas was often forced to go out of duty. Thomas loved the city but found its pace too frantic for an artist who would lay back and soak up every nuance of a street, a face, a gesture. On more than one occasion, he'd been accused of staring overlong. But the plain-faced Lord Caldwell more than made up for his impropriety with a likeable disposition. He was always readily forgiven.

The sun shone behind Elizabeth's head, just to the right, gleaming atop her perfectly swept chignon of dark brown curls. Thomas refused to let her use a bonnet, saying the play of golden sunlight on her slender features was too distracted by such a waste of material. Her gown, a simple morning dress, conservative and prim, was of a fine, luxurious blue silk. It had little adornment to its high waist and rounded skirt. A veil of cream-colored lawn crossed modestly over her breasts, hiding them from view.

He refused to let her see the portrait until he was done but she didn't mind. They only did it to pass the time away—or at least that's why Elizabeth did it. To Thomas, it was much more. His art was everything to him.

"Because when you swing your skirts fly," Lord

Caldwell teased at last, not realizing time had passed since her comment. He studied her with a most severe expression before turning back to the portrait. Elizabeth was surprised he even answered. When he worked, he got so involved that he sometimes forgot she was there. If she didn't protest, he'd make her stand still for hours. Now that she thought of it, she'd been standing still for hours.

Elizabeth's face turned a bright red at Thomas' words. Her arms rose angrily to her hips, breaking their reserved pose. "My skirts have never flown an inch above my ankles, Thomas. What a wretched thing to say to me."

"You're much too serious, dear sister," Thomas laughed, tossing his head back before he turned again to the painting. Red and brown paint smudged the rolled linen sleeve of his expensive white shirt but he didn't care. He'd ruined more than his fair share of clothing with his passion for art. To prove the point, his morning coat, abandoned nearly an hour before, was tossed carelessly on the green lawn behind him, soaking in a mud puddle. "That's precisely the reason I desire for you to stand in this exact pose. I would show the world how proper you are. As an artist, it's my duty to portray all that I see as I see it. And you, dear Elias, are standing now exactly as I see you when I close my eyes."

"Elias." The softly musing voice instantly gave her chills. She hardened herself and the half smile of affection growing on her features fell into a reserved mask. No one was allowed to call her that but her brother. Her dark eyes no longer shone as she peered coolly from her unmoving face. She instantly dropped her arms to her waist, folding them together as Thomas had instructed.

"No, no," Thomas mumbled, distracted. "Lower your chin back down. I wish you reserved not haughty."

"Such a peculiar name for a woman," the low voice continued as smooth as silk. Elizabeth did her best to ignore Harrison Rivenhall, the Earl of Wrotham. He'd come from the side door of their vast country manor, strolling about the gardens as if the estate belonged to him. She shivered to see his teasing arrogance.

It might as well be his home, Elizabeth thought in ire, for he refuses to leave it.

"Elias," the earl drew out as if tasting the word upon his firm lips just to annoy her. Harrison smiled, seeing her cheeks pale slightly at his seductive tilting of her given name. It was the only response to him that she allowed, but it was enough to encourage his further perusal of her.

Elizabeth frowned. Wrotham was a rogue through and through. If he weren't such a good friend of Thomas', she would've thrown him out a week ago when he'd arrived at the estate. Naturally, she'd heard her brother mention his good friend the earl. But, before his arrival, she'd never had the displeasure of meeting the man. Indeed, it was Elizabeth's opinion that Thomas had been way too kind in his assessment of his friend. Lord Wrotham was an uncouth, undignified, ungentlemanly gentleman who was undoubtedly only tolerated in fine society because of his title and wealth.

"I see you have deigned to bless us with your presence this morning, or should I say this afternoon, Lord Wrotham," Elizabeth stated coolly, eyeing him with the hard depths of her reserved gaze.

She hated to admit it but seeing him standing in the sunlight, bright blue eyes lazily tilted beneath his lowered lids, staring into her as if searching her soul, did something to her composure. His skin was slightly bronzed as if the sun knew him well. This man never took anything seriously, unless it was to *seriously* endeavor to annoy her. Suddenly, she wasn't so comfortable standing for Thomas with Wrotham's inspecting stare.

"Dare I ask? Were you packing your trunks to leave us? I imagine an important man such as you has many demands on his time to ever overstay his welcome in one place." It would've been a *mostly* proper observation but for the almost eager way her eyes lit when she said the words.

Harrison frowned slightly at her attempts to get rid of him. He tossed his hand with an air of indifference, though the battle sparked as his lips curled almost devilishly.

Elizabeth quivered ever so lightly to see the dimple she'd memorized in his cheek. It hadn't been the first time she'd hinted at his leaving. It wouldn't be the last.

The earl's lighter locks were grown a little too long for fashion but it only succeeded in adding to his already too potent roguish appeal. Elizabeth scowled, looking back to her brother as he worked. It annoyed her that the earl was so handsome and pleasing to the eye. She would much rather he took on the appearance of a troll. It would suit his personality better. Well, mayhap not but it would suit her distaste for him and keep her eyes off the ever so alluring build of his frame.

The earl had an ease about his appearance, a careless charm. Elizabeth liked to think of it as a laziness of dress. He carried a walking cane, though he never used it except to poke aimlessly at objects on the ground. A sapphire ring gleamed distractedly on a long finger, connected to a strong hand. Right now, the dark blue of his double-breasted jacket hung open to reveal a loosened cream tie over the high standing collar of his linen shirt. And, though his lighter vest was mostly buttoned, Elizabeth could see the play of his stomach muscles as he moved.

"Oh, do make your sister stop teasing me, Caldwell," Harrison stated dryly. He waved the hand with the cane indifferently at Elizabeth as he went to stand behind his friend. Thomas didn't notice the earl looking over his back as he worked.

"Quite right," Thomas said in distraction. "Elizabeth do stop moving your lips. I'm trying to... ah, there."

The earl shot her a superior grin at Thomas' absent-minded reprimand. Elizabeth narrowed her gaze but didn't move.

"Ah, yes, Elias," Thomas mused, pulling his brush away and stepping back from the canvas. He looked at his painting, then his sister, then to the portrait once more. Distracted, he said, "It's an unusual nickname for a lady. One doesn't hear such often."

"Father called me that the day I was born," said Elizabeth smartly. "It was because he wished to take me adventuring and knew I'd grow up as smart as any man. He did not want me limited to the constraints of my sex."

Thomas began chuckling. His eyes cleared by small measures as a grin formed on his mouth. Admitting, with much good-humor, he said, "Our father was drunk the day she was born, trying to drown out our mother's screaming. He missed the part where the midwife said she was a girl. By the time our mother had anything to say about it, he'd already informed the entire staff, and most of the countryside about the birth of his son."

"That's not what mother told me," Elizabeth protested, her cheeks flaming.

"Nevertheless, it's true. What was she going to say to you?" Thomas asked. "Monogramed baby blankets and engraved rattles began arriving for Elias. By the time she corrected your name to Elizabeth it was too late. Our father thought it hilarious and continued to call you Elias."

She didn't know why but the sultry way the earl looked at her portrait and licked his lips was having a strange effect on her. Taking the opportunity to stare at him, she let her gaze travel over his straight nose to the dimple pressed into his cheek, watching it deepen and form. A tremor hit her spine, stinging her flesh and she instantly looked away. If she hadn't been a lady, she would've cursed. What was wrong with her?

"Anyhow, I never listened to what our mother had to say," Thomas replied, truthfully. His eyes again found his painting of her and he looked almost troubled. He reached as if he would take the brush to it and then pulled back, frowning vaguely. Then, sighing, he turned and laid his brush down on the small case at his side. He was finished. "She was much too serious—just like you. I see her in you, though I hate to admit as much."

Looking at his sister's reserved features and then back at the portrait, Thomas shivered. It was uncanny. He'd done only too well a job portraying her and Thomas was usually the first to criticize his own work.

Elizabeth watched, motionless. Neither man smiled as they looked at her portrait. She wondered what was wrong. Too weak to step forward, she asked with forced lightness, "Are you finally done, Thomas? Can I move?"

Thomas merely nodded, his lips parted in a hesitant breath. He shivered again and didn't speak.

At her words, Harrison blinked and forced the lump down from his throat. When he looked over to her, the sudden haze left his playful stare and he declared, "You've captured her completely, Caldwell. Just think. If we were to hang it in the front hall and have a ball, everyone would bow to it and your sister wouldn't have to attend. Let us try it. It should be great fun to see if anyone notices if she's real or not."

"It does capture something of her, doesn't it, Harry?" Thomas said. He was the only person who called Harrison, Harry—and only rarely at that. Whispering, he said, "It's almost like I got her soul mixed up in the brush strokes."

"I daresay you must call the portrait something

besides Elizabeth. That name belongs to a playful soul," Harrison said. Seeing Elizabeth approaching, he goaded, "Perhaps, Prudence...?"

Elizabeth shot him a haughty glare. His charming smile was lost on her as was his teasing. Coming around to stand between Thomas and the earl, Elizabeth stiffened. All three stared at the portrait in silence. It definitely was her face staring out at her. But were her eyes really that somber and meticulous? Did her mouth press harshly as if she was an uninteresting bore and not a human with feelings? Was this how the world saw her as a reserved, lackluster, unexciting, perhaps even wearisome, prude?

Tears came to her eyes but Elizabeth refused to let them fall. She had too much stubborn pride for that. It was no wonder men never paid her much mind, though she was told her looks were very pretty and her slender figure pleasing. No wonder she'd not been asked to dance at balls or sought out by other women while in London last season.

Whispering low, she didn't think as she answered honestly, "I don't like how you see me, Thomas."

"I think it's precisely how you are seen, Miss Elizabeth. Brilliant Thomas." Harrison answered, still smarting from her earlier remarks about him overstaying his welcome.

The words didn't get the usual witty comeback Harrison expected. Suddenly, she turned her widened eyes to him, almost tortured in their churning depths. His words had cut her deeply. Harrison flinched, instantly wishing he could take them back. He'd never had said them if he thought she could be affected by anything that came from his mouth. Her lips trembled slightly, but she said nothing. She again found the painting, studying it.

"I'm sure you are right, my lord," Elizabeth forced calmly. There was a stiff bite to her voice. Harrison opened his mouth to speak, but he didn't know what to say. All that came to him wouldn't be appropriate to utter, especially with Thomas so near. And surely the stiff woman at his side wouldn't welcome his comfort—she barely welcomed him.

Thomas was oblivious to everything as he stared into the painted likeness of his sister's eyes. With a touch of awe, he said, "This has to be my most honest work yet."

"Yes," Elizabeth said. Then, to steal the earl's choice of words, she added, "It's truly brilliant, Thomas. It has opened my eyes. And now, having looked at it, I can't help but wish never to see it again. No one should be forced to look at how they are perceived by everyone else. It's too cruel a thing to do. There is comfort in illusions and you have crushed all of mine with this painting of yours. Oh, how I wish this portrait could show you the part of my soul that no one knows. Maybe then, I could tolerate looking at it."

Thomas' mouth fell open at his sister's hollow declaration. He moved to study her. Slowly, she nodded her head at both men, refusing to look at them directly. She was mortified beyond words at how they pictured her in their minds. Turning away to walk up the side path to the house, she didn't say another word.

Thomas looked at where his sister disappeared and then back at the painting. Swallowing, he said thoughtfully, "Perhaps she's right. I don't know that I would wish to be shown myself through other's eyes. It isn't like a mirror where you can look at what you wish and disregard the rest."

Harrison had the strangest urge to run after Elizabeth. He held himself rigid. Thomas sighed.

"Your tactics for wooing my sister leave much to be desired. It has been a week and she has not warmed to you," Thomas stated. Both men's gazes kept turning back to the portrait. Though they tried to look elsewhere, they couldn't. "Are you ready to admit you were wrong about her? That she isn't the, how did you put it? The other half of your dark, bloody heart?"

"On the contrary, seeing her reaction to this portrait only proves my point," Harrison murmured thoughtfully.

He studied the long line of Elizabeth's painted neck, the way her upper lip stretched beautifully over a full bottom one. If she'd only smile more, she'd be stunning.

Thomas frowned, confused.

"There is more to your sister than her prim exterior, Caldwell," Harrison said. "It may be buried deep, but it's there. It's what I saw in her when first I laid eyes on her, dancing unaware in a rainstorm. It's that one memory that has haunted me since. I'm hopeless. I can't be rid of her."

"I still say you are mistaken. It must have been one of the maids you witnessed," Thomas answered, unconvinced. Harrison had been pressing him for permission to court his sister for a full year. At first, Thomas thought it a joke. The very idea of the passionate earl courting his seemingly passionless sister was laughable, until Harrison became so desolate and withdrawn from the usual pleasures of his roguish life that Thomas realized his friend was quite serious.

Thomas nearly keeled over with a heart attack the moment Lord Wrotham confessed his love for Elizabeth. They were old friends. Caldwell knew him well—well enough to know when he was lying. Finally, Thomas had relented, if only to prove to Harrison that Elizabeth wasn't his type of woman. The earl hadn't even met his sister until a week ago, had never heard her speak. And

Thomas was sure that the cold slights Elizabeth had been giving Harrison all week would've been enough to dissuade him from his purpose. It hadn't. If anything, the earl only seemed more determined.

Harrison closed his eyes, remembering each detail of his unforgettable vision. Elizabeth had been in the rain, chasing after some silly kitten, trying to save it from a puddle. Her dress had been soiled and wet, clinging indecently to her slender frame. He'd been too stunned to move. She hadn't known he was there, watching her from the shadows, so close he could've touched the bodice clinging to her ripened breasts.

At the time, he'd been running away from an angry husband who was intent on having his head. Harrison had drunkenly slept with the man's wife and had no wish to take the cuckolded man's life in a duel, in addition to his dignity. Knowing he was close to Caldwell Manor, he'd gone there for sanctuary to wait out the storm before heading on to London.

That's when his life changed. Frozen, stiff with rain, he'd been contemplating waking the household. Knowing that Thomas waited in London for him kept him outside in the garden. Naturally, he'd been told that Thomas had a prudish sister whose reserved nature was legendary amongst societal circles. Even Thomas admitted his sister was tame of spirit to the point of lacking one. The knowledge hadn't prepared Harrison for what he saw.

She'd stopped right next to him on the garden path, giving up as the kitten darted away beneath a thorny bush to hide. He thought she'd have run back, huffing in anger at the darned little beast. Instead, she merely smiled, glancing over her shoulder to the house. An impish light entered her eyes as she turned to the full moon. The blue light bathed over her skin, making it seem almost translucent. The image struck him deeply. Every time he thought of it, his body would stir, his member growing so hard it pulsed with a raging fire. Harrison frowned. No matter how hard or how often he stroked it, he couldn't seem to find release. And other women held no appeal.

Elizabeth's dark hair had been wet, and she looked more like a drowned cat than a woman. But her eyes glistened in such a way and her lips spread playfully as she twirled in the moonlight, tasting the rain, embracing the storm. From that moment, it was love.

It had been over a year and, try as he might, he couldn't get her out of his head. He'd tried to forget her at first, aimlessly taking to bed any woman who'd have him. It didn't work, only lasted a few days, and soon the flavor of the world was lost to him as each night his temptress danced into his dreams.

He'd watch for her endlessly at balls and operas, looking into the distance for the sight of her, hoping for the chance at an introduction. He had endless conversations in his head with her, none of which had come to pass. She didn't go to balls and he'd missed her introduction into society. The year she came out, he'd been in Italy—tasting all the flavors of women the country had to offer. Harrison liked his women wild, naughty, feisty.

Elizabeth, by reputation, was none of those things. She was boringly proper, so prudish that even the church would surely call it a sin. She was self-aware, judging with those damnable eyes—nothing that had ever attracted him in the past. But that night, in the rain, he couldn't get it out of his head. He was obsessed.

"Ah, you take it, Harry," Thomas said at length, unaware of his friend's thoughts. "I know you're wasting your time with my sister. The dream is in your head, my friend, not reality. Take the portrait as a gift, so that you may look upon it and see the reality. I wouldn't have it upsetting Elizabeth by hanging it in her presence."

Harrison didn't move.

Turning to walk away, Thomas called, "Come, let us see what Mrs. Brown has cooked up. I'll send someone out to deliver the portrait to your guestroom."

Before moving to follow his host, the earl whispered to himself, his heart nearly to the point it could take no more of Elizabeth's rejections and slights, "I wish I could see the truth of her soul in this painting. Then, mayhap, I'd have the answer to winning her heart."

Harrison forced his eyes away and didn't look back. Slowly, he turned, following Thomas into the house.

2

THE PAINTED BROWN EYES STARED DOWN AT THE earl from the darkened corner of the Caldwell guestroom, round and piercing. The large canvas was mounted in an old frame, sitting on the floor, leaning between the wall and a decorative chair. Thomas was worried about the drying paint, so Harrison dared not cover Elizabeth's features from view. He couldn't sleep, his male member hard from looking at the line of her neck dipping to her slender shoulder, glowing in the strip of moonlight coming from the opened window.

In the dimness, she looked almost real and once his tired eyes thought to see her shift and move within the painting as if to smirk at him. It was torture, especially at night, with her so close, under the same roof, just down the hall, forty paces if he walked slow, thirty if he walked fast—not that he was counting, not that he paced the halls hoping to catch her running into the night to twirl and spin.

With a growl, he threw the crimson red coverlet off his legs and spun his bare feet around on the thick feather mattress to the floor. He didn't wear a nightshirt as was the fashion, choosing to sleep in his drawers during the winter or in the nude as was most comfortable. Tonight he was naked.

Harrison quickly looked around to the shadowed wardrobe, to the writing desk neatly folded away, the washstand, the armoire, the vanity where a crystal decanter of brandy still sat, half-drunk, next to a snifter. All the furniture matched—dark wood, ornate in curling design. Harrison barely saw it. The painted eyes of his obsession called him back to her.

Wildly, he pulled his hands through his hair, yanking the strands hard as he considered touching himself, stroking like an awkward youth to ease the ever-present tension in his loins. His eyes drifted to the painting, heating slightly with wicked ideas. His flesh burned and his arousal tightened painfully.

Never had a woman resisted his charm. He'd had it too easy in the past, he knew that now. One smile and they'd come to him. One softly whispered word and they'd spread their legs, their bodies wet and ready for him. That had been the way of it since he was a young man, just turned sixteen—perhaps even younger. But he hadn't gone to another woman for nearly a year—not since a few days after he lost his heart to a rain-soaked nymph.

Elizabeth resisted all his charm, his teasing, his goading. He'd tried every trick he'd known to get her to notice him, without being obvious of his intent. Nothing he said or did brought her a moment's pleasure. Sometimes, she'd even find excuses not to be in his presence, leaving the room as he entered it. She seemed only to take delight in his misery.

"Then you should be very pleased indeed," Harrison said to the painting. He stood, walking over to the decanter to pour a full glass of brandy. He'd tried, perhaps too hard, to break her ice, to warm her to him. It was no use. Her smiles were rare and those were reserved only for her brother. Sometimes he wondered if his rain nymph had been a dream, a hallucination caused by the storm.

"No," he said hoarsely, tossing back the whole glass at once, gulping it down to ease his suffering. Then, looking at the picture, swaying slightly on his feet, he said, "You were real. I know you were."

Harrison fell to his knees before the portrait, remembering her wet nipples, so close, so ripe, and beckoning for a kiss. Memory had perhaps added to the scene, making it more alluring to tempt him, tease him. It didn't matter. His heart was beyond lost to her.

"Tell me how to win you," he said to the portrait. He was drunk. He knew he was drunk, just as he knew he was crazily beseeching an inanimate object that could no more grant his heart's desire than the glass in his hand. "Show me anything, I implore you, Elizabeth. Give me a sign. What flower would I give to make you smile at me? What diamond? What joke to make you laugh as you did that night in the rain? What...?"

Harrison blinked, his vision blurred from drink. The moonlight seemed to quiver over the portrait, giving it a life of its own. The portrait's features were still reserved, staring out with cold, calm eyes. Elizabeth's silk clad body hadn't moved. But as he neared, he saw something peculiar. He could've sworn red roses graced the stone wall behind her back. But, now, it wasn't roses circling behind her shoulder. It was bluebells.

Harrison blinked, swallowing as he rubbed his tired eyes. The bluebells remained as vivid as the roses before them had been. Before he knew what he was doing, the earl pulled a shirt over his head and breeches over his hips. Bluebells only grew in one part of the Caldwell gardens—a hidden alcove surrounding a bench. He hurried from his bedchamber without thought. If the Fates had taken pity on him and given him a sign, he was no fool as to waste it.

23

3

Elizabeth rounded the dark moonlit path, loving the gardens at night. Her slippers crushed with little noises against the cobblestone. Night was the only time she felt as if no one watched over her. Since she was a young girl, she'd snuck from her balcony window. It was a climb she now made easily after so many years of practice, even in heavy petticoats.

Tonight she wore only her nightdress, a free-flowing gown of foulard and lace. History told her that no one would be out roaming the night and she'd felt no need to change into something more proper. The spring air was warm and a dress with numerous petticoats would be most unwelcome to her body's current freedom. Tonight, more than ever, she needed that freedom. She needed to break free from the stifling memory of that horrible work of art.

Coming to her favorite bench, she breathed deeply. The scent of delicate flowers filled the air. Bluebells were her favorite, always had been since she was a child. She liked how they carpeted the ground, spreading like a wild field of blue in the nearby woods. She'd transported some of them to her favorite bench many years ago, so she wouldn't need to go so far to see them.

Coming to her bench, she stood and looked up at the stars, smelling the flowers as only the night could stir them. Her heart poured out into the night, crying out to have the memory of the portrait erased from her. Her soul begged to be freed from the prison of herself. Her mind yelled and screamed until she wanted nothing more than to stomp her feet like a pouting child, screeching at the top of her lungs until she got her own way. She held perfectly still, not letting any of the emotions pass over her motionless, reserved face.

She didn't know how long she stood there, looking up at the heavens. Suddenly, she felt chills as if the moonlight shifted in the heavens. She blinked and the sensation disappeared.

A soft chuckle came over the night, causing her to jump in alarm. Elizabeth spun to see the earl standing, half-dressed before her, blocking her path of retreat.

Instinctively, she moved her hands to cover her improperly clad body. But as his laughter only grew at the action, she scowled, dropped her hands, and refused to be embarrassed. It was *only* the earl, after all. There was no need to take *him* seriously. He didn't even take himself seriously.

Harrison's body had stiffened in surprise to find her by the bluebells, looking up at the stars, and for a moment he was rendered speechless. He never thought his foolish dash into the night would lead him to her. At first, he thought her a vision, a ghost created by his drunken mind to taunt him.

A breeze brushed the thinness of her nightgown along her hip, rounding the curve of her butt and lovely thigh—thighs he longed to part and thrust against again and again until she screamed his name for all to hear. He swallowed nervously, his hand shaking to reach forward. Trying to think of anything that would stop his body from pouncing, he'd done the thing that came most naturally. He laughed to provoke a rise from her.

Now, seeing her eyes on him, devouring his body as he had hers moments before, he felt his stomach tighten. Her lips parted and he wanted to kiss her, to have her kiss him in many indecent ways that she would surely protest. His shaft hardened painfully and no amount of willpower could lessen its torment.

Elizabeth's lips pursed together to hide the effect he had on her. The wind suddenly felt as if it again chilled, though the breeze was warm to her flesh. Why was she beginning to shiver? Elizabeth's frown deepened in displeasure. And why did her eyes want to travel down his scantily clad body to his bare feet and back up again?

The breeze came a bit stronger than before, or was it that she was just now noticing it? His white shirt pulled to the side, hugging his muscled waist in a way that drew her gaze. For a moment, his shirt lifted and she saw the barest peek of his navel carved into the flat bed of his abdomen, over the smallest trail of hair. The sight was more intimate than she was prepared for and within that one second the image was burned into her brain.

"Have you looked your fill, Miss Elizabeth, or should I turn around for you?" Harrison smirked. He was surprised that she would allow herself the bold inspection of him. He had to admit he was pleased to discover it. If anything, it proved she did have some interest in him as a man.

Her cheeks stained a dark pink and Harrison saw her work her fingers nervously. She rolled her eyes in annoyance as she demanded, "What are you doing out here?"

"I could ask you the same thing," he mused, stepping closer.

Elizabeth stiffened at his approach and he stopped.

He wondered why it was she suddenly looked afraid of him. Her eyes narrowed, holding him back. He knew she was too proud to run away though her body looked tense and ready to do so.

"This is my home," she said, lifting her chin regally to stare down her nose at him. If he hadn't known differently, he'd have thought her title above his. "I, unlike some, actually live and belong here."

"You don't like me much, do you, Elizabeth?" he asked, not letting his hurt show in his light words. Each time she tried to get rid of him, it cut him deeply. His only desire in life was to be near her. He longed to make her happy, for her happiness would complete him.

"You will address me properly, my lord," she ground out, not looking pleased. Her eyes narrowed and her tone cut. "You may be my brother's good friend but you are not mine. I haven't given you leave to be so familiar with me. In the past week, I have tried to overlook some of your more glaring faults but I can no longer permit your vulgarities in—"

"Tell me, *Miss* Elizabeth," Harrison broke in with a quick wit, if only to stop her onslaught of words. His brain didn't want to hear them. After living with her in his head for the last year, he didn't feel as if they were strangers. "Did you memorize Lady Hatfield's entire book of etiquette or just the first three chapters?"

Harrison's whole body lit with fire. Her skin against the moonlight was so pale and blue. He wanted to kiss the long line of her neck. Her hair was still pulled back, ever proper. He wanted to tug at it until the locks swam over her shoulders in waves that he could touch. It was clear she had absolutely no idea of his affection for her.

Elizabeth's mouth gaped as a wave of pain assaulted her senses. The earl was too smug, looking at her in his superior way. She wanted to cry out. It was he who invaded her sanctuary. This was the only time she had to be free of prying eyes and damning judgments. He could never understand how it was for a woman—the eyes of society constantly on her, watching her, waiting for her to make a mistake. He was a man and society was much more lenient on a wealthy, handsome gentleman.

But here he was, invading her sanctuary, calling her a prude. The memory of the portrait haunted her. She hadn't seen it since its conception and she didn't wish to look on it ever again. She hoped Thomas burned the horrible thing. If he did, it wouldn't matter. The image would forever haunt her.

"I'm surprised you are even aware that such a book exists, Lord Wrotham, being as it wasn't written in a playbill with large print," she quipped. She was unaware of how their sparring made her chest heave against the fabric of her nightdress, or how the breeze pushed the thin material to every single curve of her body as she faced him.

His voice dipped, low and seductive, the words hoarse from the passion he always carried for her. "So I'm not your friend, Miss Elizabeth?"

Elizabeth blinked, wondering at his tone. If she weren't mistaken, he looked hurt by the idea. Saying the only thing she could think of, the only thing that might get his eyes from sending chills over her flesh, she said, "I don't make fast friends, my lord, and I have only known you for a week."

"What if I told you I have known you for much longer?" he murmured, stepping even closer. He lifted his hand as if he would reach for her. Elizabeth jerked back but didn't step away. There was something in the softening depths of his eyes that held her where she was. His hand hovered near her face, lingering as if trying to decide its next course. In the end, he pulled it away.

Eyeing him warily, she replied in her confusion, "You mean you have heard Thomas speak of me and feel as if you know me?"

Harrison, realizing the words that slipped past his lips, nodded. It wouldn't do to tell her how he obsessed about her. No doubt, she would only ridicule and torture him for it. He licked his lips, not answering.

"After seeing Thomas' idea of me earlier today, I

don't think you can know me at all from his descriptions," she said, never knowing why she would admit to such a thing—especially to the Earl of Wrotham.

Suddenly, the earl blinked as if coming from a fog. "I'm sorry to hear that we are not friends, Miss Elizabeth."

"Why is that?" she asked breathlessly. She became all too aware of the heat from his chest. The playfulness entered his eyes once more, calling out to her to join him in a fight—or was it something else he tried to wrest from her? The breeze molded the linen of his loose shirt about his muscular frame. She saw the folds of his tight physique beneath the weak barrier. She itched to touch him, to pull his shirt up to see if her memory of his stomach was accurate in its amazing detail. She smelled him, a scent so intoxicating in its subtleness that it drowned out her notion of the flowers.

"For if you were my friend, I would be honor bound to keep your secret. But, being as I'm not, I'm honor bound to your brother to tell it." Harrison bowed properly at her and moved away.

Her gaze drifted down to his muscular backside, before stopping. "Wait. What secret do you speak of?"

Harrison smiled at her worried tone. Covering his grin with a look of innocence, he turned back. "Why, the secret of you being out in the gardens, at night, un-chaperoned, clad only in an alluring nightdress. If one were to see such a thing, imagine what would be assumed of it."

Alluring? Elizabeth glanced down at her body. He thought her nightdress was alluring? Then, the rest of what he said penetrated.

"You wouldn't dare to tell him." Elizabeth cried, rushing forward only to stop and back away from him once more. "Not like that. When you say it in such a way, it sounds... *horrible.*"

"Is it not horrible? And so very indecent of you, my most proper Miss Elizabeth Blakeney?" he murmured.

Her gaze appeared troubled and she didn't notice that he again came to her. When he looked at her, his gaze strayed to her lips. She shivered.

"Why do you keep tormenting me?" she asked. "What have I done to deserve it? Are you so bored that you must find ways to vex me to ease your own... lack of amusements?"

"Do I torment you?" Harrison asked, drawing ever so closer. He wondered if he could even begin to torment her a fraction of how she plagued him. Her nightdress stirred, blowing forward to touch his legs. He almost shivered to feel the touch of it pressed so airily to him. Aside from the gloved hand she'd offered him upon meeting, it was the closest she'd ever willingly come to him. He didn't need to touch her skin to know how it would feel against his. Hours of dreaming had brought her flesh to him, soft as silk, smooth as velvet, warm as fresh cream.

"Yes," Elizabeth returned instantly. Her eyes found his, so close, so bright, so full of humor beneath their depths. But there was more, a look she'd never realized in him. His dimple pressed deeper, though it wasn't with a playful grin. He looked almost serious. "You call me a prude. I'm not a prude."

"Then kiss me," he stated, staring at her parted lips as they formed words in her sultry voice. He stiffened, wondering what made him say the words in his head as he waited breathlessly for her answer.

"What?" she gasped, sure she imagined his request. Oh, why did her mind choose now, this man, to bewilder her with?

"You must let me have a kiss, if you wish me to keep your secret," he said. He lifted his hand to touch her cheek, ever so gentle as he stroked over the softness of her skin. He'd been wrong. It felt better than he dreamt it to be. "Come, Miss Elizabeth, what's a kiss between friends? Give me an act of trust."

Elizabeth hesitated. She didn't move, didn't answer.

"No? Shall I call your brother?" Harrison asked as he made a move to leave.

"No, wait, don't," she stammered. Taking a deep

breath, she eyed him with disbelief. Her gaze filtered to his mouth, not at all repulsed by the idea. A strange awakening came to her senses, fogging her brain with the idea of such a simple, wicked pleasure. "All you want is one kiss? That's it? Nothing else?"

Harrison stiffened. His whole body was aflame being this close to her. No, he wanted much more from her than a kiss. In a whisper he answered, his voice trembling ever so slightly, "Yes, just a kiss."

Elizabeth didn't hear his hesitance over the beating of her own heart. She kept her eyes trained on him for any deceit as she turned her cheek so that he may peck her. She was surprised when he didn't take it.

"Your promise first that you won't stop me," Harrison said.

Elizabeth smelled the liquor and thought he played a game merely to toy with her. The melodious tone of his voice washed over her. His breathing noticeably deepened and she wondered at it. A thrill coursed through her. It seemed to jump off him as she felt his heated breath on her neck.

"You have it, so long as you don't tell Thomas you found me out here—so long as you don't tell anyone about this," she answered. "If you do, I'll deny it."

Harrison shuddered to think what Thomas would do to him if he found out he was indecently propositioning his sister. It would be the end of their friendship for sure —or at least the near end of it.

"On that you have my word," he murmured. To his delight, he watched a tremor race along her body.

"All right, you may have a kiss, my lord." Again she offered her cheek. "You have my promise that I won't stop you."

He drew his fingers across her offered cheek, only to turn her lips to him. His eyes narrowed, serious and probing as he commanded, "Lay down on the bench."

When she opened her mouth to protest, his finger moved over her lips to hush her. Her mouth trembled along his finger. Her eyes grew wide, until Harrison thought he saw stars reflecting in their dark depths.

"I've been known to make a lady's knees go weak. I wouldn't want you to fall," he teased.

"I don't swoon so easily, I assure you," she quipped, though her voice was softer than usual. "Pray, take your kiss and end this. I'm tired and wish to get some rest. Some of us awaken with the dawn, not hours after it."

"Are you afraid?" he goaded. "Are you so like your portrait?"

A strong sense of danger overcame her usual hesitance. It was the only thing he could've said to get her down on the bench. Detecting the challenge, she wanted desperately to prove that she could be devious and spontaneous, that she wasn't like the damning portrait.

Elizabeth sat, her back stiff as she waited for him to come to her. He didn't join her. Instead, he stood to tower over her, indecently close. She saw his stomach near her face. There was a protrusion coming from his breeches but she didn't dare to dwell on it.

Swallowing, she said, "Well, take your kiss. I assure you, my knees feel perfectly fine. I won't fall over."

Harrison swiftly knelt before her. Elizabeth blinked. Her pulse raced and she had the insane notion he was about to propose marriage. When he didn't take up her hand, she relaxed.

"I said, lie down," he commanded her.

"I'm fine—"

"You are afraid, aren't you?" he forced, guilted by the fact that he had to resort to coercion to bend her to his will.

"I'm not afraid of you, my lord," she answered, cool and reserved. It was a lie—a damnably huge lie. Elizabeth feared this man greatly. She feared the way she felt when he looked at her. She feared the insincerity in him, legendary in his conquering reputation. He was a gentleman rogue. He used women, left them. She didn't want to admit to it before now but had been trying so hard to deny she even liked him. The first moment she saw his eyes, alighting on her as he stepped down from his fancy carriage, she'd felt it—a jolt, a sting, a swift and powerful burning deep inside, a void needing to be filled. She was drawn to the rogue and she hated it.

She'd done her damnedest to slight him, ignore him, and spurn him. In return he teased her until she wanted to rip out his hair. He took nothing seriously, so it only stood to reason he didn't take her seriously—nor the things he said to her. Any day she expected one of the prettier maids to walk by and catch his eye, drawing his attention away from her. That day hadn't come yet, but she had no doubt it would.

Elizabeth kept her eyes steadily on him. Maybe it was the way the moonlight caressed his tight features, or the slight shadowing of a beard on his normally smooth face, that convinced her to disregard societal rules and mores. Slowly, she lay down, crossing her hands on her stomach.

Harrison had dreamt of this often, her soft body lying down for him willingly, vulnerable to him, so close that he could touch it. A curling smile flickered over his devilish lips, dimpling his cheek. Her dark eyes looked up into his. Her face was bathed by moonlight, her gaze shining with the mesmerizing depth of the starry night. How easy it would be to climb atop her, pressing her legs open so he may feel her most intimate of secrets. He wondered if he would find her thighs wet with her body's response, or would he have to coax the reaction from her, stroking her with his tongue.

His gaze drifted languidly over her form, liking the way her arms pulled the gown to her chest, outlining it. He moved his hand to her stomach as he leaned forward. His palm skidded across to her hip, holding her down as he leaned his mouth closer, closer.

Harrison waited to hear her scream in fright, waiting for her flailing hands to hit upon his head and knock him away. She didn't move. Emboldened, he opened his mouth, trailing his tongue along her bottom lip. She didn't budge, didn't flinch or blink as she stared into his eyes.

Elizabeth froze. His fingers were warm as they moved against her, kneading lightly into her flesh, touching her as no man had ever tried. The first brush of him to her mouth was soft, testing.

She wasn't sure what she was supposed to do. She'd expected a brief peck, not this hot sensation of lava to her core. For a moment, she thought he'd killed her. Her heart nearly stopped as his hand traveled boldly over her hip, wrapping his long fingers to the bottom curve of her backside. A soft moan sounded and Elizabeth blinked, realizing it escaped from her lips.

Harrison heard the feminine sound. It called to his

soul, making him mindless in the knowledge that she felt something between them and that his obsession for her, his longing, wasn't completely one-sided. The rogue inside him couldn't stop, having been suppressed for so long. His free hand delved into her hair, gripping her jaw tightly to keep her lips to his. He deepened his kiss, burning his raging need into her mouth as he whispered her name softly against her tongue. He thrust beyond the barrier of her teeth. His mouth moved, passionate and wild as he tried to taste every moment, every breath, every crevice of her sweet mouth. So long he'd wanted her and so long he'd suffered.

With a mind of its own, his fingers instinctively glided along her leg, inching the material of her night-dress up. He was pleased to find the naked flesh of her warm thigh beneath his searching palm. He couldn't stop, didn't even think to try. Why should he stop? It's what he wanted and she didn't scream, didn't fight him.

Elizabeth's eyes shot open in surprise. She'd been enjoying the onslaught of his massaging tongue to hers, reveling in the peculiar movement and the sensations it wrought. But, to feel his hand gliding beneath her gown, circling her hip, his thumb dipping along the inner edge to... to touch...

"What do you think you are doing," demanded Elizabeth in a hush, breaking away from the kiss to gulp for breath. She slapped him as hard as she could, leaving an imprint on his face as she knocked him back.

Harrison landed hard on the grating cobblestone, blinking in surprise at the assault. He'd been in a mindless web of ecstasy, his member hard and ready to go on. Becoming aware of what he'd done, he could only smile to see her running away from him.

Looking down at his culprit hand, the one that dared to press into the soft petals of her heated center, he groaned. She'd been wet for him and so very hot. Nothing could turn him away from wooing her now. He closed his eyes, breathing deeply of the bluebells—his new favorite flower.

Elizabeth would be his.

4

Elizabeth was shaken as she made her way back to her bedroom. She nearly fell from the trellis as she scaled the side of the country home to her balcony. Her heart pounded frantically, but she didn't care. She had to get away from the earl.

Closing the large double doors to her balcony, she pulled the drapes firmly over them as if they alone could keep all that had happened outside in the night. It didn't work. The feelings Lord Wrotham stirred were still there, running a rampant course over her flesh—as wild and untamed as the rogue himself.

Rushing to a long, freestanding mirror, next to her vanity of oak, Elizabeth paused. A bit shy, she looked herself over to see if she was altered in any way. She stared at her lips for so long they looked swollen—probably from her biting them to get out the sting of the earl's kiss. No one had ever dared kiss her before, not like that.

Finally convinced that her face was still her own, she pulled her nightdress back to look at her body. Glancing down the front, she blushed and instantly dropped the nightdress down. She couldn't believe he had actually touched her there. She couldn't believe that she liked it. A flush hit her features and she felt a curious heat all over her body.

Elizabeth glanced at the window, her mind beginning to churn in consideration.

A man like the earl would have no qualms about telling what they did together. She wouldn't, couldn't become one of his conquests.

With a dive, she hopped into her large bed and snuggled deep into the covers. Elizabeth pulled the blanket over the back of her head. She stared out, unmoving in their apprehension until she could no longer stay awake.

THE MORNING LIGHT SHONE THROUGH HARRISON'S bedroom, alighting on the red walls like they were on fire. Moaning, he rubbed his lips. His tongue was thick and dry from drinking and stuck in his mouth so he could barely move it. His eyes were rimmed with red. Yawning, he suddenly sat up, scratching the back of his head. A myriad of memories came back to him, making his body lurch with excitement.

He hardly dared to dream it was real. Elizabeth had let him kiss her. He looked down at his hand, remembering all of it in perfect detail. Then, frowning, he pulled the covers from his body. He tried to ignore the constant nagging of his erection. The damned thing never seemed to go away. Then, realizing he still wore his breeches and shirt from the night before, he moved to look at the portrait. Surely, that had been the only falsity in the night.

Harrison laughed at himself for his whimsy, and then suddenly, he stopped. He blinked several times as he stared at the painting. The roses were still gone, replaced by the bluebells. He explained this away as an oversight, knowing he'd been staring so hard at the woman that he could've mistaken the type of flowers painted beside her.

Chuckling, he went to the washstand and began bathing himself in the clean water. As if a portrait could reveal a woman's soul to him. The very idea was laughable. He'd have to remember to take it easy on the brandy in the future.

He dressed quickly, flipping his wet hair to let it dry naturally as he did every morning. Tugging on a dark blue frock coat, which he knew brought out his eyes to brilliance, he said offhandedly, "Tell me, wise portrait. How shall I make Elizabeth converse with me today? No doubt she'll be angry at my kissing her."

Harrison grabbed his boots, slipping the dark leather over his feet. Looking to the portrait from where he sat before it on a chair, he froze. The color drained from his features as he tugged the last boot over his foot. Standing, he crossed over to painting. Now he knew he wasn't imagining things. Next to the stone wall leaned a riding crop.

Harrison's eyes widened, looking up to the stillness of Elizabeth's face. He must indeed be going mad, for her eyes did seem to sparkle with a hint of mischief. Studying the picture carefully, he memorized every detail. Then, turning his back on it, he asked, "What shall we do when we ride, I wonder?"

He waited several seconds, his hands trembling slightly. Then, turning about, he carefully looked it over again. Nothing had changed.

Still not convinced the riding crop wasn't magically perceived, Harrison strode from the guestroom. He would test this strange occurrence for himself—scientifically—and ask Miss Elizabeth for a ride.

6

Elizabeth tried to meet her brother's gaze but couldn't. A horrible blush stained her cheeks and wouldn't go away.

Thomas had tried several times to catch her gaze from across the table but she was more interested in pushing the fruit around on her plate. He felt terrible about the portrait and thought perhaps she was sore at him for having created it.

"Elizabeth—" he began, only to stop when she turned to him. Her mouth opened as if to speak at the same moment. He bowed his head for her to go first.

"I wanted to tell you I was going for a ride this morning," Elizabeth said. In truth, she wanted to avoid the earl at all cost. "I did not want you to worry if I wasn't about."

"Oh?" Thomas said, pondering her words.

Elizabeth often reported to him, though he never demanded it from her. She was much too proper and reserved for him to take much care in her whereabouts. Perhaps as her guardian, he was too lenient with her. But she was his only family. He loved and trusted her. Not much could happen to her in the surrounding countryside.

Glad that she at least started to form a smile in his direction, he nodded his head in concurrence. "I think that is a fabulous idea. Would that I could go with you but Mr. Turner arrives today from London. He wishes me to approve..."

Thomas waved his hand, not wanting to mention the paintings Turner came to collect. Elizabeth turned her gaze down as her expression fell. The very idea of Mr. Turner exhibiting her likeness for all of London's fine society to gawk at left her breathless.

"I won't be giving him that one," Thomas said, softly, seeing her discomfort. Elizabeth nodded quickly, not answering otherwise. Changing the subject, he said, "Where shall you ride to?"

"The old cottage ruins, I think. I love the bridge this time of year," she answered, smiling. "Someday, you must promise to come and paint it for me. So when I'm too old to seat a horse, I may look at it every day and remember my youth."

Thomas nodded, pleased to see that she wasn't taking his painting of her too hard. "That's a promise. Though the ruins are far away. Should I call for a groom to accompany you?"

"Beautiful morning," Harrison called striding into the dining room, a wide smile on his roguishly handsome features.

Elizabeth averted her gaze in mortification as she turned back to her plate. What was he doing awake so early? She'd planned on being far away from the manor when he showed himself. Horrified, she refused to look at him.

"Ah, Harry, so glad you could join us," Thomas answered pleasantly, not noticing his sister's discomfort as she slighted his friend with her silence.

"Caldwell." Harrison nodded. Then, turning to Elizabeth, he said, "Miss Elizabeth."

"Lord Wrotham," she mumbled darkly, her lips tight. Her gaze fixed before her.

"I hoped to borrow one of your horses today, Caldwell. The groom tells me mine is still sore from getting trapped in that sinkhole when we raced over the fields the other day," the earl said, studying Elizabeth out of the side of his eyes. She hadn't moved, not even to glance around.

"Ah, perfect," Thomas exclaimed. "Mr. Turner is

here today so I can't go but Elizabeth requires an escort to the old cottage ruins. Would you mind terribly taking her and keeping her out of trouble?"

"I'm never in trouble," Elizabeth stated loudly. When both men looked at her, one with a set of mischievous bright eyes that begged to differ, she lowered her tone. "What I mean to say is that surely Lord Wrotham has other plans and I don't wish to impose upon him."

"No," the earl said before Thomas could inquire into such, much to her growing ire. Harrison saw Thomas' small smile and knew he'd purposefully given him the opportunity to spend some time alone with his sister. Harrison almost felt guilty for the trust Thomas had in him.

Elizabeth's rounded eyes pleaded with the earl to stop talking. He only smiled back, his dimple forming next to his firm lips to distract her. Elizabeth remembered the feel of those lips all too well. Her mouth stung with the promise in his eyes, the knowledge.

"I've no plans at all. I would be most happy to act as your chaperone, Miss Elizabeth," the earl continued. Elizabeth frowned.

"Wonderful." Thomas glanced curiously at his pale sister. "Are you sure you're up for a ride today? You appear as if you are getting ill."

Elizabeth saw the look that came over the earl's

features, daring her to run away scared. Her jaw lifted regally. She wouldn't let this man get the best of her.

"I'm perfectly well, completely unaffected," she answered. Harrison frowned at that. She smiled, her cheeks becoming almost rosy as she stood in victory. "You are such an artist, dear brother. It must be the light that makes you take note of such things."

"Forgive me for worrying," he said. Both gentlemen stood as she did. Thomas leaned over to kiss her cheek, relieved to see a slight shine back in her pretty features. "Why don't you take a picnic lunch with you? The weather is fine for it and I won't be of any company today. You should stay a long time and enjoy the afternoon."

Elizabeth wondered if she should remind her brother about the impropriety of such a thing. Unwed ladies didn't picnic alone with roguish gentlemen. However, knowing they were the only manor for miles, she doubted anyone would see them. Then, seeing the smirking grin forming on the earl's lips as if he could read her thoughts, she held quiet. So much for her newest plan to make it a quick ride there and an even faster ride back. Before he even said a word, Elizabeth already knew the earl's answer.

"Marvelous idea, Caldwell," Harrison said. "I'll ask the grooms to ready the horses."

Meeting his stare dead on, battle lighting in her eyes, Elizabeth answered tightly, "And I'll ask the cook for the picnic."

The men waited as Elizabeth walked from the dining room. Thomas sat back down, taking a sip of tea without touching his plate. Then, looking at the earl, he shook his head sadly.

"You still haven't given up your dream?" Thomas asked, not expecting an answer. He saw the earl's face when he looked at his sister. There was hope in the man's features. "I had hoped the portrait would show you the truth. I see I was mistaken."

"The portrait has shown me plenty," Harrison said enigmatically. Thomas didn't catch his tone. "You only must ask it the right questions."

"You mean ask yourself the right questions when looking at it," corrected Thomas.

The earl grinned, coming out of his thoughts. He didn't know how the painting worked or to what end but the magic of it was helping him to woo his heart's desire and he wouldn't question it. It was what it was and he would leave it at that.

"Yes, naturally," the earl said with ease, unwilling to reveal the painting's secret to his friend. "I meant you must ask of yourself. Whoever heard of talking to a painting?"

7

"WHAT EXACTLY DO YOU THINK YOU ARE DOING?" Elizabeth snapped when they were mounted and well away from the earshot of the grooms. Her dark green riding-dress splayed over the horse's back, her legs crossed properly to one side. The gown was simplistic, fitted to her body for ease of movement. On her hands were thick leather gloves, to protect her delicate skin from callusing against the reins. Her eyes flashed with fire when she glanced at the earl.

"What?" Harrison asked dryly, though his eyes sparkled with devilish mischief. "Am I not seated as a proper gentleman?"

He looked down to where his large thighs gripped the horse's saddle. Elizabeth's gaze automatically followed downward to look at his legs strained against his tight breeches. Catching herself, she forced her gaze over the distance, leading her horse slowly up the drive to the side gate.

"You know what I speak of," she said under her breath as if the passing shrubs could hear them. She rode beside him along the edge of the garden to the nearby field that would take them to the ruins. The horse's hooves clopped steadily on the cobblestone, mingling with the sweet songs of birds and the hum of insects.

"No, Miss Elizabeth, I'm afraid I don't," he responded, his face keeping the mask of pleasant confusion. "Pray tell, explain it to me."

"Why did you volunteer to ride with me today?" she inquired, rounding her eyes to him and letting the horse guide itself over the tall grasses. Her stare gave nothing away. "And I know it was you who left those bluebells by my door this morning."

"I don't deny it," he answered lightly, his gaze full of ease and charm. Harrison smiled, letting his gaze roam over the back of her neck, loving the way she shivered at his attention. He lazily let his hand drift through the air as he barely gripped his reins. "What sort of gentlemen wouldn't thank a lady for—?"

"Don't you dare to think that last night meant aught —" she tried to interrupt.

"Last night?" he inquired in forced amazement. His

bright eyes lit with teasing as he said nonchalantly, "I meant your hospitality in letting me stay in your home. Oh, I see, you refer to when you were on your back, begging me to kiss you?"

Her cheeks flamed. In her anger, she spurred her mount slightly faster. "That's not what happened and you know it."

"Are you afraid I'll kiss you again?" he inquired, his eyes shooting sparks in her direction. He couldn't help himself, knowing she responded as she did. This morning she was shaken. He'd seen her try to draw away when he'd offered his hand to help her mount. He affected her. Harrison couldn't let such a sweet revelation go. It gave him hope.

"You won't," she proclaimed, giving him her most haughty look.

He ignored her words, grinning like a devil. Neither one of them noticed the beauty of the fine spring morning nor the warmth of the rising sun as it shone over the distant hills, dancing within the rolling grasses and wildflowers. His hot eyes pierced her with meaning as he looked to her mouth.

"Are you afraid you'll want me to kiss you again, Miss Elizabeth? Do you not trust yourself to be alone with me?" Harrison's voice lowered into a seductive murmur, meant to send chills over her spine. It didn't fail.

Elizabeth turned her eyes forward away from the heat of his bold stare. It wasn't fair. No man should have eyes such as his, or lips that still burned her with their memory. Her tone noticeably upset, she said, "If you can't speak politely, my lord, you shouldn't speak at all."

Elizabeth kicked her dark brown mare firmly in the side, spurring it forward. Her cheeks were flushed with heat and her heart pounded wildly. She didn't know what promises the earl's gaze spoke of when he looked at her but to her everlasting shame, she was more than curious to find out.

Harrison chuckled to himself, urging his horse behind hers. He stayed slightly back, only to watch her round bottom as it bounced in a steady rhythm on her seat. A smile came to his lips and he groaned inwardly. His body was on constant fire, made worse by her nearness. His lids dropped lazily over his eyes as he thought, *if only she would seat me as easily as she does her mare. What I wouldn't give to have her ride me in such a way.*

Harrison's sigh was audible.

Elizabeth directed a withering glare at him. Then, shaking her head in noticeable exasperation, she leaned forward, racing across the field to get as far away from him as possible.

8

Elizabeth never managed to get very far ahead of the earl as she galloped over the field to the cottage ruins. She normally loved the freedom of a spirited ride. However as Lord Wrotham stayed behind her back where she couldn't keep a wary eye on him but could only hear him, she found herself stiff. She wondered what he looked at, what he thought about as he looked. The very idea unnerved her greatly.

Harrison watched Elizabeth's backside with delight, mesmerized by the movements of her hips, her arms. Such wickedly sinful thoughts came to mind as they rode. A smile came to his lips, lingering with a longing that reflected in his gaze. By the time the ruins came into view, a half of an hour later, his body was hard and his mind was fogged with many indelicacies.

Elizabeth reined her horse, sitting tall as she slowed it to a stop. She looked over the clearing, waiting for the earl to join her. The sky was bright and blue with little puffy clouds forming like cotton. Blue reminded her of the earl's eyes and she looked away.

A small stream cut through the field, flowing under an old stone bridge overgrown with ivy. Flowers dotted the landscape and, in the distance, just beyond the small wooded grove were the black spots of cows out to pasture.

"So, where is this cottage?" the earl asked, looking around. He didn't see anything but nature and the beauty of the woman next to him. His gaze stayed with the woman.

Elizabeth nodded to the grove, edging her horse forward until she saw a dilapidated wall of stone marking the backside of the abandoned home. Motioning her gloved hand in the direction of the trees, she said, "There."

Harrison eased his horse inappropriately close to Elizabeth's mount. Not looking to where she directed, she said, "Ah, I see."

Elizabeth shivered, leaning away from his voice. When she faced him, he was so close to her that her lips nearly brushed his cheek. Her breath caught in her throat as she felt his warmth hovering over her skin. She knew she should pull away but her legs wouldn't move, her waist wouldn't bend.

Her legs tensed along her mount's side. The horse's head bounced slightly as if he sensed her discomfort. Feeling the earl's breath along her neck, streaming in hot waves over her skin, she delicately trembled. To her amazement, and strange disappointment, he didn't touch her.

Harrison pulled away, seeing the goosebumps he'd drawn over her smooth skin. His tone low and soft, he asked, "Shall we explore it?"

"It wouldn't be wise," Elizabeth said, blushing slightly as she turned back to the cottage to avoid looking at him. His smell had somehow drifted over her and now she could breathe in nothing else.

"Because it's falling to ruin?" he inquired, still not looking at the stone wall. The way the sunlight shone atop her dark hair made him desperate to touch it. He wanted to run his fingers over her sunbathed skin—every inch of it as he parted her from her very proper clothes. He wondered what it would be like to make love to her on the grassy field, surrounded by such beauty. When he closed his eyes, he could almost imagine what his name would sound like passionately moaned from her trembling lips.

Elizabeth didn't need to look at the earl to bring

every detail of him to mind. He was again dressed care-lessly as if he tossed his clothes over his all-too-fine body while walking out the door. He didn't wear gloves to protect his hands. She couldn't help but wonder if his palms would be callused. And what would they feel like pressed against her skin?

He's a rogue, she scolded herself, wondering how one kiss could keep affecting her judgment. *It's not like he means anything by it. He's only toying with me, trying to seduce me out of boredom because there is no one else.*

The thought strengthened her resolve. Belatedly, she answered, "No, because it's said to be haunted."

"Oh, how very intriguing," Harrison said, his eyes sparkling as they always did when he was around her. His eyes were finally on the stone and not her back. "Now we simply must go in."

"Have you no sense of caution?" she asked him, surprised by his eager tone. His gaze seemed to devour her. Had his gaze always been like that? Was she now noticing it because of what happened between them?

"Have you no sense of adventure?" he demanded in return. "How many times have you been riding out here?"

"Countless," Elizabeth answered guardedly, wondering what he was getting at. "Ever since I was a young girl, Thomas and I would venture here. My father used to bring us riding along this very path before he died."

"And in those countless times, how many times have you explored that little cottage?" he inquired, already knowing her answer.

"Never," she said, almost ashamed. "I have never been in it."

"You can't tell me it's because in all that time you've never wanted to see it." Harrison swung off his horse, leaving the reins hanging free so that the animal could graze. Coming around to her side, he lifted his arms to help her down.

"What are you doing?" she asked, nervous excitement shooting through her like stout liquor.

"I simply can't sit back and allow you to be so careful all your life, Elizabeth."

"Miss Eliz—" she began to correct him. His look stopped her. He frowned gravely at her.

"So help me," the earl stated as if to himself, before letting go of a heavy sigh. "It's now my sworn duty to make sure you experience more of your world and we are starting with that cottage."

Elizabeth felt a strange sensation coming over her at his words, though she knew better than to take anything the earl said seriously.

Harrison saw the desire in her, the need for something more. So help him, he was going to help her find that something more. It may be the only way he'd help her to come around and finding some sort of feeling for a man like him. He had tried but he would never be molded into her idea of a perfect gentleman. Sure, he was respected and well liked. Rumors surrounded his name but were never taken too seriously, and if they were, he was forgiven for them.

Harrison knew that opening her up to new possibilities would be the only way they could be together. If he didn't, she'd marry the most proper, most insufferable bore she could find and she would live out her days miserable and yearning. He couldn't stand for her to make that mistake. She deserved happiness and laughter. She deserved to smile. She had such a lovely smile, a smile that could skip the beating in his heart. But she never used it, never turned its radiance on him. So help him that was going to change.

"But, my brother," she began as he kept her gloved hand forcibly in his large palm and began dragging her to a narrow path in the woods.

"Ah, hang your brother and hang your stubborn sense of propriety," Harrison mumbled good-naturedly. Suddenly, he stopped.

Elizabeth was propelled forward by his pull and she landed close to his solid chest. When she tried to push back, his arms wrapped around her narrow waist and held her still.

Elizabeth gasped, her eyes instantly rising to the earl's steadfast gaze. He was so close. His muscles moved along the backs of her arms. She smelled his fresh, clean scent. He was warm, so warm, and suddenly she was freezing and in need of his heat. One dip of his head and his mouth could claim hers. Oh, how she wanted it to. A rush jolted through her as if she was struck by lightning. If he didn't hold her up, she would've swooned at his feet.

Harrison was pleased when she didn't pull back. A slow smile found his lips as he said to her, "Whether you like it or not, I'm your friend Elizabeth. As your friend, I say life is too short to live in fear as you do. You are so young, so lovely. There is no reason you shouldn't experience that loveliness and youth while you have it. If you don't live a little, I fear that one day you will regret never having enjoyed these years. By then it will be too late. Your body will be old, your looks gone. What will you do then? Pine away for lost chances? I refuse to let that happen to you. I simply wouldn't be able to bear it."

"I'm not afraid," she protested nervously. "I don't live in fear."

"Ah but don't you see, you are afraid," he said. He touched her, liking the feel of her against him. He'd longed desperately to hold her, needed it so much. He knew for certain that she belonged forever in his arms, just as he knew she didn't realize it yet. "You hide behind your mask of propriety, only doing what you're told you must do. Don't you ever wish to do what you want to do? Don't you ever want to break free and fulfill your own desires? Don't you want to feel every feeling there is? Don't you wish to realize and enjoy every desire, every whim?"

Elizabeth trembled. It was as if he was reading a part of her that she didn't dare look at until that moment when it was pointed out. The breeze blew her gown up over her ankles. A draft worked its way up her skirt to give her a heady caress.

"If people see you as that portrait, let them. But it doesn't mean you are that portrait," he put forth, seeing he had her rapt attention. "You don't have to be the woman your brother painted if you don't want to. We all wear masks to the world, Elizabeth. They don't define us. Only we can define ourselves. I say to hell with society and their double standards. They don't have to know anything we don't tell them. So long as you're discreet, you can have everything."

"How can I trust you?" she asked, stirred beyond measure by his seductive words. "Your speech sounds practiced."

"You probably can't trust me," he answered honestly, thinking of his ulterior motives. Almost guiltily, he let her go. Keeping her hand in his, he continued to the cottage.

Elizabeth shivered, thinking of all he said. He was right. Life was too short. She wasn't an emotionless painting, she had never been. It was her mother's constant nagging and tutoring that had drummed her reserved nature into her being. It was as if the woman had given her daughter hope, that her father believed in her and gave her a man's name, only to take it away by insisting she act the impeccable lady.

Something clicked within her, a wildness that surged with delight that she finally stopped to listen to it. It was her heart, beating frantically, trying to escape her chest with the burning desire to do as the earl urged.

She could have both the painting and the life. Let the world think what they must, she wanted them to. What better ruse for society to embrace than her as a prude? What better cover for all the misdeeds she could discover and learn? Eyeing the earl's backside with a renewed sense of purpose, Elizabeth knew she'd found the perfect instructor.

9

THE RUINS OF THE OLD COTTAGE WERE SET IN THE shadows of the woods. Elizabeth had never been so close to the old stone and her body jolted with a sense of alarm and excitement. She pulled closer to the earl, who stiffened to feel her next to him. Looking down over his shoulder, he saw her worried face but also the newfound sparkle in her eyes.

"Are you afraid?" he asked.

"Yes." She nodded. "Go inside."

Harrison kept his pace slow as he walked over the overgrown forest floor to the front door. The piece of wood hung on the frame, eaten away by weather and time. When he touched it, the door fell inward. Elizabeth jumped at the loud noise and started to giggle. Harrison shot her a boyish grin over his shoulder.

"Shall we wake the ghosts?" he asked, his eyes narrowing with mischief. Elizabeth nodded. Harrison looked down over the threshold. The old door was in the way and he stepped onto it. Gallantly, he instructed, "Watch your step."

Elizabeth let him lead her into a small, dusty room. Their boots creaked on the old floorboards. An antiquated stone fireplace with a collapsed chimney sat along the back wall of chipped stone. A broken table, an abandoned pot and some shattered plates littered the area. Cobwebs danced in the rafters, drifting in the slight stir their presence caused.

Thin rays of sunlight managed to filter into the dark atmosphere of the one room cottage. Out of all her daydreams of it, Elizabeth never thought it would look so ordinary or plain. She frowned.

Harrison, seeing the look, asked, "Disappointed?"

"Yes," she answered truthfully. "Ghosts aren't very tidy creatures, are they?"

The earl chuckled, nodding in agreement as he eyed the rafters. He could detect a dusty nest but no birds. He turned around to look at her again as he spoke. "Shall I escort you back outsi—?"

Elizabeth couldn't stop herself as she acted on pure instinct. When she saw his lips, parted in speech, she leapt forward and pressed her mouth to his. Harrison inhaled in sharp surprise but instinctively wound his arms around her to keep them from tumbling over to the dirty floorboards. She moaned lightly against him. She pressed her fingers into his shoulders, gripping him for support. When he was too stunned to return her hard, closed mouth kiss, she pulled back.

"I've never done this before," she said, glancing with innocent longing at his unmoving mouth. Her cheeks were flushed, but she refused to let them stain with embarrassment. Her heart hammered in her chest as she stared deeply into his amazing eyes. Almost shyly, she said, "You'll have to tell me what to do."

A groan left his throat as he dipped forward. Instantly, his tongue darted over the rim of her mouth, parting her lips. She didn't stop him, drowning in the pleasurable sensations his lips brought to her senses. His mouth moved against hers, searing her with his expert tongue, massaging and exploring.

Elizabeth's body felt as if it was on fire. She instinctively sucked his tongue gently into her mouth and was rewarded with a small moan from Harrison's lips. Her stomach flipped in nervous excitement. It seemed so wicked and wrong, against everything she'd ever learned. But she couldn't stop. Her head spun with his earlier words.

You don't have to be the woman your brother painted

if you don't want to. We all wear masks to the world, Elizabeth. They don't define us. Only we can define ourselves. I say to hell with society and their double standards. They don't have to know anything we don't tell them. So long as you're discreet, you can have everything.

Oh, how Elizabeth wanted to have everything. She wanted to feel, to be explored. She wanted to taste things and see things and do things. She wanted to live, to feel as if she were alive—despite that society would frown upon her kissing her brother's best friend in an abandoned cottage. Society didn't live her life for her, not anymore. She wouldn't live in fear of their judgment. She'd be careful, sure as not to bring shame to Thomas and herself but she would no longer be afraid.

Elizabeth moaned. She ran her hands down to explore his chest. Pulling back to breathe, she dipped her fingers under his jacket, trying her best to push it off his broad shoulders. "You're right. I have been drifting in a horrible state of rules and decorum. I haven't been living at all. I want to live, my lord. And I want you to show me how."

She tried to kiss him again, her mouth swollen and wet from his teachings. Harrison pulled back. His body ached with a burning desire for her. He hadn't meant for her to throw herself at him like this. He was stunned beyond belief that she would come to him so readily, so boldly. It excited him, made his flesh tighten and throb, fuller than he could ever remember it being.

"I didn't mean," he began, setting her back so he could think straight. He saw the cloudy, dazed look in her dark eyes, and he saw the dreamy smile coming to her lips. To their mutual surprise, he stepped back, away from her when she would reach for him again. He tried to turn away, to lead her back out into the sunlight but she bit her lip in such a thoughtful pose that his body lurched and he couldn't move. All he could do was stare at her.

"I want you to take off your clothes," she announced, looking him over. Her eyes sparkled with anticipation as they settled on the foreign bulge between his legs. Her body wiggled beneath her binding corset. "I want to see what a man looks like naked."

"Elizabeth, I didn't mean for you to do this," he tried to deny her and yet was tempted to obey her request. His mind tried to reason with him, with her. "I meant for you to explore this cottage—"

"Do it," she said, her eyes darkening. "Or are you the one who is now afraid? What holds you back? Whose rules do you follow?"

Harrison didn't move, wondering what sort of monster he had inadvertently created. He refused to be goaded by her. One of them must keep a logical head. He was surprised to find out that it was he who would do so.

He thought of Thomas, his good friend, his best friend. Thomas trusted him with his sister. Harrison promised before ever meeting her that he wouldn't treat her like the other women he'd pursued. He wanted what he created with her to be honorable, pure, forever. Now, looking into her eyes, he knew that more than anything he wanted her happiness. He would do anything for her, regardless of the cost.

"Fine," she stated when he thought too long and said nothing. Elizabeth was too giddy in her newfound freedom to catch his hesitance or his honorable intentions. Why should she be any different from the women he seduced? She knew what she asked him and accepted it. A man like the earl would never love anyone but himself. So she wouldn't love him in return. She would enjoy him—fully. Her eyes lowered beneath the set of her thick lashes. "I'll go first."

Before Harrison could even find the words to stop her, her fingers pulled the fastening of her bodice. Within seconds, she had the dark green material pushed down around her ankles into the dirt and was stepping out of it. Standing before him in a petticoat and corset, she smiled almost shyly at him.

Harrison's eyes were on her breasts, untouched by

the sun, untouched by everything and everyone. The rounded globes pushed up indecently from a row of lace and silk. All it would take was the flick of his finger, or of his tongue, to draw the tip out for his viewing.

Elizabeth found herself growing excited as unfamiliar sensations coursed through her. She liked the daring way he looked at her, staring with his lips parted, his breath panting.

She drew her long fingers to her waist, pulling the tie of her petticoat free. His body hardened as she stepped out of it. Clad only in her long silk drawers, that was so thin he could see the dark curls between her thighs, and the enticing corset that latched in the front, she smiled up at him. The expectant look on her face, unseen to him before that moment, stole his breath.

Elizabeth unconsciously trampled her gown as she walked over it to get to him. He didn't move. Slowly her arms wrapped around his neck, pressing her near naked body to his hot length. She gasped to feel the most obvious of their differences pressing between them. She didn't pull away.

Harrison was surprised. His size usually intimidated the most experienced of women—until he showed them he knew how to wield such power properly.

"Do I please you, my lord? Will you not say aught to me?" she asked, bold and shy at the same time. Her lips were offered to him and she stared directly into his. She trembled along his length. "Will you not kiss me?"

"Do you know what you ask for?" he said down to her. He trailed his hands over her slender arm. She shivered, drawing closer as her head fell back. "Do you understand what you wish for me to do?"

"Yes," she breathed. It was a lie. She had no idea what she was asking. She only knew that she wanted it more than anything.

"If we do this, I'll be forced to marry you," he said, not against the idea but oddly excited by it.

"No," she said back, drawing her arms along him. "You won't."

Harrison stiffened in disappointment. His eyes narrowed. "Your brother will—"

"—will never know," she broke in. She dipped her eyes to look at his chest and she drew lazy circles around the base of his neck. "I won't tell him. You won't tell him. No one will ever know of this, except us."

"You don't understand what you're asking of me," he tried. "You risk too much."

"I know that my body has the strangest urge to feel you. Please, my lord, touch me. Kiss me. I want you to, desperately," she pleaded with a feminine sigh that drove him mad. "Don't you want...?"

Harrison tried to pull away but the look of her softly

clad skin combined with the almost hurt plea of her words was more than his fervent body could resist. Instantly, he dipped his head to taste her offered lips. His kiss claimed and conquered her mouth, stealing her breath and her mind. He became forceful, shrugging from his jacket before lifting her and spinning her to the fireplace to press her back into the hard stone.

Once trapped, he drew his fingers intimately between her thighs, searing her through the silk that guarded her most intimate opening from him. Her body was damp and flooded him at that first touch. With a growl, he ordered, "Is this where you burn for me?"

"Yes," Elizabeth said, dizzy from the feel of his bold fingers pressed against her. Her body convulsed against him, tightening slightly as it throbbed.

Harrison's lips lowered to devour her neck, her face, her chest. He flicked his tongue over the top edge of her corset, reaching a dark nipple, hardening the bud with his suckling lips. Her body jerked, desire fanning everywhere in her at once, stemming from his hot mouth on her chest. She felt alive. She took hold of him, kneading his linen shirt in her hands, grasping at his shoulders for support.

The hand between her thighs didn't move, though her body wanted it to. Harrison kept his hand steady, feeling her gentle pulse, gauging her reaction to him, feeling what made her body jolt with desire as he took his time discovering her.

"Ah, my lord," she whimpered, her voice growing louder. Her hips pushed against his cupping palm, not knowing what it was she sought. She wiggled against him, instinctively knowing he held the key to her release. She wanted what he could give her. "Ah, yes."

His thumb dipped into her corset to free the other imprisoned bud. He massaged her breast in his palm, causing lightning to shoot through her. Harrison smiled, delighting in her feminine shivers. His lips drew hot kisses along her neck, biting her earlobe, licking her pulse beat. He delighted in the little sounds she made, urging him on, begging for more, whimpering in her newly discovered desire.

Elizabeth squirmed, searching against the warm palm that waited between her thighs. Harrison grinned, feeling her heat beneath his instruction. The silk clung to her hot opening, sticking in the moisture pooling from her body onto her thighs.

"I'm going to kiss you," he said near her mouth.

She leaned her lips up and forward, offering them to him.

"No," he denied, his hand lifting to cover her lips. A finger dipped in the corner, near her teeth and he pulled her jaw open so his breath panted into her. Feverishly, he whispered into her mouth, "Not these lips."

Elizabeth blinked, confused.

"These lips," he murmured, a finger stroking up into her. She called out in surprise as wave after wave of agonizing pleasure shot up into her. He massaged her, intimately pressing into her heat, so gentle and firm, keeping a slow rhythm.

Before she could comprehend what he meant to do, Harrison was on his knees before her. He found her slender hips and jerked the silk drawers down her legs, leaving her in nothing but her tantalizingly erotic corset.

His mouth watered to see the soft mound of hair waiting for him. There was nothing to keep him from drinking the sweet nectar from her body. He smelled her perfume, tempting him forward so that he might fully taste her. He pulled her thighs apart from behind to accommodate his lips.

Elizabeth gasped and looked down to see his head dipping to touch her. She watched his lips move, extending as they puckered toward her most private area. She raised her hand, ready to swat him back if what he attempted felt too peculiar. But as his tongue drew from between his teeth, the erotic sight nearly did her in and she leaned back into the stone wall. She gripped her hands behind her head, searching for support, finally finding it on the old fireplace mantle.

Harrison groaned. His lips latched onto her, sucking the little nub of her desire between his lips. His teeth nipped gently. She tasted sweet as he sipped from her body. Elizabeth gasped, her hand fell into his hair. Instead of pushing him away, she pulled him closer.

Harrison growled in pleasure as she thrust her hips toward his mouth. It was such a natural response as was the growing wetness against his tongue. Her parted thighs quivered against him. Her hips wiggled and jerked, hitting his nose as she tried to understand what was happening to her. With a groan, he gripped her tighter. Forcing her body open, he drew her leg over his shoulder.

Harrison chuckled in greedy passion as the action opened her body completely to him. Her fingers were in his hair, pulling and pushing frantically as she sought her first release. He traced his tongue over the edge of her opening, swirling and sucking at the top arch, lapping and dipping along the soft velvet lips before thrusting into the center hold.

Harrison gripped a breast, thumbing over her ripe nipple. Elizabeth cried out, her hips finally discovering a mad rhythm as his tongue darted erotic and bold inside her feminine lips. His growls of approval hit her in vibrating waves, weakening her knees. Her leg tightened over his back until she sought to smother him with her body.

"Oh my... *lord*," she cried.

Tremors racked over her as she climaxed hard into his parted lips.

Harrison moaned in ecstasy. He didn't stop, even when she pushed at his head to get him away. He forced her to ride out her passion, sucking greedy and hard until every last drop of her was spent and released.

Pulling back, he let her leg slide off his shoulder onto the floor. He licked his lips. Her climax had been perfection and he reveled in the memory of her tremors against his lips. She gasped for air. Her nipples strained as they reached out to him, inadvertently begging for more. Her eyes were dazed with wonderment and a soft, confused smile graced her panting lips.

"Oh, oh," was all Elizabeth could manage, over and over again. "Oh, my, oh."

Harrison caught her up into his arms when she would have fallen to the floor like a rag doll. She shuddered lightly in the aftermath of his touch. Nuzzling her neck, he said, "I warned you my kisses could weaken your knees."

"Ah," she moaned, his expert lips giving her chills. Her mind conceded to that point wholeheartedly.

"And now I'll show you another way to get such feelings," he said, nipping at her ear. "I'm going to fu—"

"Elizabeth? Harry?"

Elizabeth stiffened. Her eyes widened as she blinked herself back into reality. Weakly, she said, "Thomas."

"Get dressed," Harrison said as he sprang into action.

"Lord Wrotham?" Thomas called. "Where are you hiding? Elizabeth?"

Elizabeth tugged on her drawers, rushing to grab her petticoat. Her limbs trembled, which made dressing hard. Harrison waited with her gown. After she had the petticoat laced, he eased her dress quickly over her head. As Elizabeth moved to tie it into place, the earl dipped his fingers down her bodice and pressed her nipples back into the corset. She shivered at the touch, pausing to look at him.

Harrison couldn't stop himself from pressing a quick kiss to her lips. "Be quick."

Elizabeth tasted herself on his mouth and it gave her a jolt of wayward pleasure, a heady sensation as if they'd gotten away with something devious. She laced her riding-dress as Harrison smoothed his appearance. His body was still hard with unfulfilled desires but there was nothing they could do about it now. He had the promise of later to sustain him. He'd waited a year for her and he could wait a while longer. He ran his fingers quickly through his hair, before tugging her to the cottage door.

"Elizabeth?"

"Caldwell quit your hollering," the earl called, leaning over to dust off Elizabeth's skirt. Her eyes still had a slightly dazed, dreamy look to them that was very out of place for her. "We are here."

"Where? I don't see you," came the reply.

Harrison shot Elizabeth a grin that seared her to her toes. She trembled, stumbling when she tried to walk. Her whole body hummed.

"By the cottage," the earl yelled, not daring to touch her. "Elizabeth tripped and has dirtied her gown. I think she might have twisted her ankle."

Elizabeth frowned.

"It explains your soiled gown," the earl said. "Now, if you know what's best for you, get to limping."

Elizabeth couldn't help her secretive smile as she began to hobble. Grabbing his arm for support, she called, "Here, Thomas. I'm all right."

The earl led her over the dirt path to the sunlight. Thomas sat astride his white horse. His eyes narrowed to see her slightly disheveled state and flushed cheeks. His tone full of concern, he swung off his mount and demanded, "What happened?"

"I tripped on a floorboard," Elizabeth said. "I finally

got the nerve to see the cottage and a bird... I thought it was a spirit."

Her tone sounded so dejected that even Harrison believed her story, and he'd been there.

"Ah, well, let's get you home then, shall we?" Thomas said, offering his arm to his limping sister. Both men helped her onto her horse. Then, they mounted up to join her.

"What are you doing here, Thomas? I thought you were meeting with Mr. Turner." Elizabeth gave her brother a sweet smile. To Harrison's disappointment, she ignored him as she rode beside Thomas.

"I was going to join you at the picnic. Mr. Turner sent word that he wouldn't be here until tonight. He's been delayed in London," Thomas answered.

As they made the trip home, Elizabeth didn't deign to speak to Lord Wrotham again. Harrison's pleasure in the day soon faded as he realized she had no intention of acknowledging him before her brother. In fact, she acted as if nothing had changed between them at all.

10

Elizabeth's cold treatment of the earl lasted the rest of the day, much to Harrison's dismay. They ate the picnic lunch in the Caldwell gardens, spreading out blankets on the lawn. Thomas spoke of his paintings, keeping his sister's rapt attention most of the afternoon.

Harrison watched her in amazement, especially when it became clear that she was going to continue greeting his comments in the same fashion she'd always had—like he was a nuisance not worthy of her time or patience. He'd expected her to soften toward him a little, to shoot him a secretive glance, a feminine blush. Nothing. She barely looked at him.

By the time evening came, Harrison found himself in a dismal mood. If he didn't have the memory of her trembling body on his tongue and lips, he would never have believed anything happened. But, the memory of her on his mouth was burned so deeply, he could think of little else, couldn't even taste the wine without thinking of drinking of her instead.

Turning to look at the fire, Harrison ignored the London paper he'd been pretending to read. He glanced across the masculine study to the bookshelf. He usually found some diversion in books but not even the idea of the most ribald of comedies was lightening his spirit.

Thomas had gone with Mr. Turner, cloistered in Lord Caldwell's art studio. Harrison knew from experience that the men wouldn't emerge from there any time soon. The earl knew that he could join the men, had been invited to do so but he didn't wish to sit back and listen to them argue as they forgot he was there. They spoke of art—something artists loved to do—and would be oblivious to everyone and everything else until all their points were settled.

"There you are."

Harrison stiffened, instantly turning around to look over his shoulder. Elizabeth shut the study door behind her, careful to keep quiet as the door latched. Harrison frowned, wondering if she mistook him for Thomas in the dim light of the fireplace. He had turned off the gas lamps, liking the dark for his sulking.

"Your brother is in his workshop, Miss Elizabeth,"

Harrison said coldly. After a day spent being slighted by her, he was in no mood to have his heart trampled anew.

Elizabeth turned to him at his low words. To the earl's surprise, she smiled shyly at him. His heart nearly stopped beating. She was so beautiful. Carefully, she bit her lip as she came forward.

"I know," she said. "I just left there. They will be busy for most of the night, I'm afraid."

Harrison eyed her as she came forward, wondering at the look on her face when she neared him. To his surprise, she stood by his chair instead of moving to sit. A light flush came over her skin.

"I wanted to see you," she said quietly.

That admission caught him off-guard and he was hesitant to feel any pleasure from it. His brow lifted as if to say, *Oh?*

"I wanted to talk to you about what happened this morning," she continued.

Unable to stop himself, Harrison lifted his fingers, gliding the backs of them over her forearm and wrist in a lazy movement. He was surprised when she shivered but didn't back away from him. He waited for her to tell him it was a mistake and it couldn't happen again.

To his amazement, she knelt on the floor beside his chair, looking up at him, her dark eyes framed by the long length of her lashes. Her arm drew along his thigh as she faced him, resting ever so intimately but not moving.

"I wanted to say I was sorry we were interrupted," she said, her gaze dipping down, moving along his chest to where his arousal grew. That's when he noticed her gown. She'd changed her dress from earlier and now wore an evening gown with a low bodice. His gaze roamed her cleavage, turned golden from the fire. He moved his fingers over her arm, testing as he lightly dragged them over her exposed chest.

Elizabeth shivered. A small smile came to her features. She closed her eyes and leaned forward, allowing him access to her body. Her breasts heaved as a heavy sigh left her lips. He didn't move, save for his leisurely dancing fingers as he carefully watched her reaction. He turned his hand, moving up to cup her jaw in his large palm.

"You could've fooled me," he said, before letting her go. He purposefully turned his gaze back to the fireplace. He had to look at anything but her sultry lips, begging for kisses. "The way you've treated me today."

Was he hurt? Elizabeth blinked in surprise. Was he pouting? Suddenly, she giggled.

Harrison stiffened.

"It was your idea to fool society and do what I wanted in private," she answered. "What would you have me do? Proclaim our actions to my brother? He would demand a marriage, you said so yourself. And at the cottage you were as frantic as I, no more so, to hide what we'd been about. I thought you'd understand."

Her explanation made sense. But it didn't excuse her cold slights and hard looks, or her sharp jabs at his person in front of others.

"I thought we had an arrangement between us," Elizabeth said. "No one would ever know about what we do."

Harrison frowned. This wasn't turning out as he'd hoped. He didn't want to be her dirty little secret she hid from the world. He wanted to be more to her, for she was much more to him.

Elizabeth bit her lip. She turned to sit on his lap. The earl stiffened, not moving to feel her as her body lowered on top of his. She laid the back of her head on his shoulder. His chest pressed along her spine. She liked the strong and protective feel of his hard body to hers.

Elizabeth longed to have his arms wrapped around her. She wanted him to hold her, touch her, kiss her. Her stomach twinged and throbbed, growing hot at the memory of his lips against it. Already she was addicted, wanting to feel him on her again. She knew she shouldn't trust him but she did. She trusted him with her body, wanted him to teach her what he knew, wanted him to share his worldly experience with her. No one had ever struck her interest as he had. No one would ever be the perfect instructor. She'd never be able to trust anyone else. The earl would keep her secret, if only for his friendship to Thomas.

"Get up," Harrison ordered.

A strand of her hair tickled his jaw. She smelled so good, so fresh and clean. His fingers itched to touch her. His hard flesh longed to plunge into her, staking his claim. He wanted to stick himself in every opening she had until she knew she was branded as his woman. However, his ego still smarted from her careless dismissal of him all day and that kept him from acting.

Elizabeth trembled, thinking he meant to show her something new. She instantly stood. Harrison stood behind her. His eyes closed, his resolve wavering slightly.

"My lord?" she asked when he didn't move to touch her. She glanced over her shoulder at him. She looked so vulnerable. He couldn't say what was on his mind, couldn't confront her about it.

"A servant may come," he said at last. "I ordered a cigar. It's not safe to play here."

"Then where shall we play?" she asked.

Harrison smiled at her eager tone. Shivers of plea-sure ran along her spine at his look. Slowly, he bowed to her, turned, and walked away.

Harrison paced the length of his bedroom, grinding his bare feet into the carpet as he tried not to look at Elizabeth's portrait. His body sung with the idea that she ignored him all day because she wasn't sure how to receive him after such an experience at his hands. Undoubtedly, she didn't understand all that happened between them—how amazing her response to him was and his to hers, how special. And, when they were alone, she did seem eager to be with him, to learn from him, to please him. It was more than he could've hoped for.

It was quite possible that it was his own unfulfilled desires that made him so sensitive to her treatment of him earlier in the day. He knew his body ached for her in such an unbearable way and that he could've drawn more from her actions than she intended. Perhaps she had looked at him tenderly like she did in the study. It was possible, in his preoccupation with the need for release, that he'd missed it.

Going to the window, he looked out over the night and mused, "Tell me, portrait, where should I next encounter Elizabeth?"

His heart sped slightly as he took a deep breath. He turned, looking the painting over. His eyes narrowed as he crept forward, trying to see in the dim cast of moonlight. The riding crop was there as were the bluebells. He'd checked the broken wall in the garden earlier and indeed it was red roses that grew—clear evidence that the portrait had indeed changed.

Looking at it now, he saw no difference. He frowned, wondering if he was missing something. Then, hearing a light knock on his door, he stood. Glancing around, he went to the dresser and pulled a bottom drawer. Jerking a blanket through the air, he tossed it over the portrait to hide it from view. Then, crossing over in quick strides, he answered the summons.

As he opened the door, Elizabeth looked at him. She wore her nightdress, her long, dark brown hair flowing over her shoulders in gentle waves. Glancing over the hall to make sure she was unwatched, she pushed him out of her way as she stepped into his room. The door shut quietly behind her and she leaned against it. Her chest heaved with barely contained excitement as she looked at him. Her full bottom lip sucked between her teeth, giving evidence to her fear and excitement.

"Elizabeth," he began, his tone full of wonder and question that she would dare to come to his room.

Elizabeth continued biting her bottom lip, glancing up at him. She swallowed, nervous about being alone with him now that she was there. She'd thought about him all day, though she would hate to admit the content of those thoughts to him. She'd softened somewhat to his charm, though she thoroughly convinced herself that it was a physical attraction only.

Elizabeth knew that he was a rogue with many lovers. He would undoubtedly discard her when he was done but only if she didn't discard him first. She was smart, logical. She knew this wasn't love between them but lust. Who knew lust could feel so good? Before now, she never realized why someone would risk everything for a chance at a moment's pleasure.

When he didn't continue, Elizabeth stared up at him. "Do you want me to go?"

"It depends," he murmured, drawn to her. He saw why she was there. It was written on her lovely face. He knew she'd come so he could finish what they started in the cottage. He placed his hand over her head and leaned into the door.

"Depends, my lord?" she asked, weakened by his nearness.

"Yes, on what you've come here for," he finished. His eyes pierced into her, awaiting an answer.

Elizabeth shivered. He loomed over her, towering above her with his impressively broad shoulders and firm lips. She loved those lips, loved what he did to her with them.

"I came to see if you would kiss me again," she said softly. "If you wanted... to..."

"Only a kiss?" Harrison drew forward so she could feel the heat from his body soaking into hers, though he didn't touch her.

Elizabeth's mouth went dry at his sultry tone. She pressed back into the door, breathing heavily. He wore a linen shirt, pulled out at the waist, unbuttoned on the top. She could see the smoothness of his chest, the hard muscles peeking out at her. The shirt ends hung over his tight breeches hiding his hips from view, hiding the mysterious bulge that captured most of her imagination. His strong feet were bare.

She looked past him to the fireplace. No fire burned, so the room was dark. Only the bright moonlight from outside gave relief to the shadows. It cast over his body, making him appear wickedly alluring. She trembled, wanting to see all of him. Her heart beat faster. This affair was dangerous and it thrilled her beyond measure.

"I," Elizabeth tried to answer. Nothing came out, so she nodded.

"Oh," he answered. Leaning over her, Harrison pecked a quick kiss on her cheek and pulled away. "There, now you've had a goodnight kiss. Pleasant dreams, Miss Elizabeth."

Elizabeth's eyes widened when his hand dropped and he backed away from her, still watching her. Her mouth fell open. There was a teasing light in his expression.

"I'm sorry," he said, his handsome face tilting quizzically to the side when she didn't move from her spot against the door but merely gaped at him in surprise. "Was there something else you wanted?"

"Well," she began, confused. Suddenly, her gaze dipped down to the carpet.

Elizabeth was mortified. She shook her head and turned to go, unable to face him. Her eyes teared as she searched blindly for the door handle.

Harrison saw her look and rushed forward to stop her, reminding himself that she was new to such games as these. She stiffened when he placed a hand near her head, palm flat against the dark wood, keeping her from leaving. He pulsed with need and there was no way he was letting her from his room until his desire was fulfilled.

Coming forward, he pressed his heavy manhood into the small of her back, forcing her hard against the door. She gasped as a jolt of sensation crowded her being. Her breasts pressed into the unforgiving oak, not nearly as unyielding as the man behind her. She took her fingers from the latch, rising on the wood in a slow caress. His chest trapped her to his as he let her feel every curve of him overpowering her.

Leaning close to her ear, he said hotly, "Are you sure there was nothing else you searched for tonight?"

Elizabeth tried to speak but the feel of Harrison's tongue trailing over the rim of her ear stopped her. He let his body push into her, let her feel his strength as he did delightful things to her ear. He pressed his hands flat to the wood, not moving to touch her. Her body was so soft. With a bend of his knees he could've ground his readied manhood into the cleft of her buttocks. He let it press near the small of her back. She shivered and he grinned to himself in pleasure.

"Tell me, Elizabeth," he demanded, pulling her lobe between his lips and sucking gently. "Tell me the real reason you came to my room tonight."

"I wanted," she breathed, before whispering honestly, "I wanted you to teach me what you know."

"Ah," he murmured, biting the lobe gently.

Harrison smiled. He liked his women bold. If he were to be her instructor, she would learn that as her first lesson. He would make her say the words to him. He would make her beg. His arousal pulsed in instant protest of the plan, wanting to surge forward and conquer that instant, trying to tell him that her coming to him was enough. He concentrated, tempering his desire back. He couldn't act rash, lest she not beg to remain in his bed.

"I want to live while I'm young, like you said," Elizabeth said as if reading his thoughts. She shivered. His attention to that one ear made the rest of her body very jealous. She closed her eyes. "I don't want any more regrets. I don't want my life to resemble that horrible portrait. I want to have secrets. I want to have mystery. I want to feel. I want you to touch me like you did this morning."

The last was said in such a light pant that he had to strain to hear it. A wave of pleasure and longing mixed in him until his need was painful.

Slowly, he drew his hand down, pulling her long hair off to the side to expose the back of her neck to his lips. When he kissed her there, she cried out lightly, shivering all over. Harrison drew back, amazed at her reaction to such a simple caress. He tried it again, licking lightly down her spine. Again she trembled violently, whimpering as he kissed the bend where her neck met her shoulder. She worked her hands into the door.

Nipping her gently, he murmured, "Do you like that?"

"Ah, yes," she said too weak to think. When he kissed her there, it was almost as pleasurable as when he'd kissed her between her thighs. Her body was heating to the point of boiling. She felt every flex of his muscular form against her. Her mind was drawn down to the firmness of him against her lower back.

Harrison released her, stepping away. She blinked, suddenly feeling very cold now that his body was gone. She turned, looking up at him. He'd drawn back far enough that she had to step forward to touch him.

"May I look at you?" she asked, her eyes dipping over him. Her blood was rampaging with the passion he created.

He held out his hands wide, offering himself up for her inspection, unashamed and so confident it made her limbs shake. His eyes pierced into her and a crooked smile came to his devilishly handsome face.

Elizabeth went to him. Her gaze devoured his perfect form. Slowly, looking deep into his eyes, she moved her trembling fingers to his chest to unveil him to her, unbuttoning his shirt. His look didn't waver. He didn't lower his hands in the slightest to stop her as she tugged the linen from his shoulders. She swallowed, looking down at the folds of his chest.

He was dark against her lighter skin and as she touched him, his breath deepened in approval. She explored with her fingers where her gaze led, over his shoulders, to his sides, up the center from navel to neck. The small, dark nipples drew her attention and she moved to touch one. To her surprise, it budded beneath her caress. A low moan came from him and his body jerked. She glanced up to see his eyes were tightly closed.

"Kiss me there," he demanded in a whisper, not looking at her.

Elizabeth leaned forward, her hands sliding to hold his hips. She lightly puckered her lips around the nipple in a gentle kiss.

His body jerked, and he said hoarsely, "Lick me there."

Her tongue darted out to drag over the tender bud. She was rewarded with another deeply satisfied moan. Going to the other side, she gave his other nipple the same soft treatment, enjoying the texture in her mouth, liking the taste of him.

Elizabeth pulled back, smiling and feeling very powerful. Her gaze traveled down his firm stomach.

When she glanced back up, he was staring at her, the smile gone from his face. His gaze smoldered her with its heat.

Slowly, she continued to undress him, dropping the breeches to slide down his legs. She gasped, pulling slightly back to see what he looked like. She looked up, puzzled. He chuckled as her mouth opened to ask a question only to close in confusion.

Elizabeth glanced over his hair-roughened thighs and calves, only to draw back to his center. A strange curiosity flooded her as she looked at his long, thick erection. She was no fool, knowing that there were differences between them and she'd felt that difference as he pressed into her. She didn't expect it to be of such a grand size.

"How do you hide it under your clothes?" she asked, awed, surprised she'd never noticed it poking out like it did at this moment. She wanted to ask him to step over to the moonlight so she could get a better look.

Harrison would've laughed, if she didn't sound so serious. Trying to keep a straight face, he answered, "It's not always like this."

She blinked, confused.

"It grows when it wants to be petted," he teased, knowing she didn't understand the joke.

Elizabeth smiled and he almost lost himself right

there as she nodded, thinking to understand. She came forward, cupping her hand around him as she stoked his arousal with light fingers, petting it to see what would happen.

Her breath deepened. She didn't allow her hands to tarry long as they moved from his shaft to explore his hips. She stepped around him, eager to see and feel all of him. His tight buttocks flexed attractively in the moonlight, making her shiver. Instantly, she ran her hands over his spine, his shoulders and arms, gliding down over the backs of his thighs. There was no measure of fat on his handsome frame, only the soft rippling of toned muscles —not so significant as to be obscene but definitely there beneath the surface.

When it appeared her exploration of him was going to go on forever, Harrison reached behind his back and pulled her forcibly around to face him. He kicked his pants from his ankles as he drew her before his chest.

"Now, my turn," he said huskily.

Elizabeth's eyes widened as he leaned over to lift her nightdress from her. In one quick swoop, she was naked. Her first reaction was to cover herself, though it was pointless after what he'd done to her that morning in the cottage and with what he was going to do to her tonight— what she wanted him to do.

"Tsk, tsk," he scolded, drawing her arms down to her

sides and away from her breasts. He leaned to kiss her shoulder and she jerked with the pleasurable sensation. The reaction fascinated him. Whispering, he said, "It's my turn. Hold still."

He drew his fingers up her arms, exploring her with bold strokes over her flesh. He teased her breasts, rubbing them, cupping them, avoiding the centers, which budded instantly in protest of the neglect. He trailed his hands over her hips, gently swooping over her curves. Her skin was so soft, addicting. He cupped her buttocks, squeezing hard, spreading her open ever so slightly.

"Ah," she gasped, taking a sharp breath when he did it again. She never knew her flesh could be so sensitive. Fire burned everywhere, pooling in her hips until she was sure she would explode if he didn't take his lips to her body once more.

"Very lovely," he said to her. Licking his lips, he added, "So beautiful."

Her arms reached for his neck, wanting to draw him down between her thighs. He kissed her mouth in a bold, passionate sweep of the tongue. He tweaked her breasts, giving the center peaks attention at last.

"Oh, Lord Wrotham," she gasped, trying to push on his shoulders to get him to his knees.

Harrison growled, leaning to take a breast in his mouth, sucking at it deeply.

"Please, I can't take this," she pleaded, pushing harder.

"Mm," he groaned into her chest. Pulling away, he looked at her. "I'm not letting you leave. Not until I've had all of you. There is no escape for either of us."

She trembled to hear the possessiveness in his words but didn't have time to wonder at them. "No, please, do what you did this morning... kiss me again. Please, it aches."

Her cheeks colored slightly as he got her meaning. He chuckled, a dark and pleasurable sound.

"Where?" he asked playfully. He took his fingers to her and pressed them intimately into her slick opening. He was delighted to find her extremely wet and ready for him. If ever there was a doubt about her having passion, the moisture won the debate. "Here?"

"Ah, yes," she cried, trying her best to thrust against his hand.

Harrison instantly crushed her lips with his to silence her scream. His eyes widened as it was muffled into his mouth. He drew his fingers back.

"You have to try to be quiet," he said in a soft voice when she quieted to a mumbling protest. "Or you will call the whole house to us."

Elizabeth bit her lip. Her eyes dipped as if in apology.

"Ah, never be sorry for it," he growled into her, going to kiss her again and again in a tender onslaught between words. "I like that I can make you scream. Now, get in my bed so I can better explore you. I'm going to show you that there is much more pleasure to be had than a simple kiss."

Elizabeth's body pulsed with life. She didn't want to leave him, even if it was to crawl into the large bed. Taking a deep breath, she did as he commanded.

Harrison strolled after her as she hastened across the floor. Elizabeth threw back the red coverlet and crawled in. By the time she turned around, he was coming in after her. She didn't bother to pull the covers up. The night was warm and his body seemed to radiate a heat all its own.

Elizabeth rose to meet him before he was fully to her. Her lips parted to kiss his. They knelt before each other, their lips joined, their bodies searching and pressing together. Harrison grabbed her fingers, drawing them down to his arousal, desperate to have her stroke him.

"Touch me here," he growled to her lips. He guided her hands back and forth over his smooth length. "Ah, yes, like that."

He forced her on her back, licking her breasts, devouring them as he sucked the buds deeply into his mouth. Her hand fell away from him, unable to reach as he drew his mouth lower. He licked her navel and her back arched. Her hips searched for him.

Harrison drew his finger to part her opening. His eyes were steamy as he watched her thrash about. He rubbed her, circling her swollen lips and nub with precision. She panted for him, sighing and moaning at what he did. When he felt her body begin to tremble, he pulled back.

Elizabeth moaned in protest. Harrison worked his mouth against her flesh, kissing and nibbling eagerly along her body, until he was above her once more. His arousal ached with a fiery need only she could meet. His hands were on her legs, spreading her for him. He knew her body was ready, had tasted her desire.

He hesitated only slightly as he brought himself to her. She was so exquisite, sprawled willingly beneath him. For a moment, he wondered if he was insane, wondered if his mind had finally taken pity on him and given him an illusion he could hold.

"I have to warn you," he said into her ear, desperate not to miss his chance. Hope built with each passing second. He kissed her neck, sending chills over her body. "This might hurt, being that it's your first time."

"Mm," Elizabeth moaned, her eyes closed. His body overwhelmed until she could feel nothing but the man before her. "I don't care. I need you."

Elizabeth didn't realize what she said to him, her lips continued to moan and pant incoherent thoughts. Her body stirred to such a pitch that she was sure he killed her and she didn't care. Her legs worked restlessly against him, begging in a way her mind could not.

Harrison brought himself to her, driven by every fiber in his being to join them. He wanted her so badly he almost cried.

Elizabeth didn't notice, too drawn up in her own thoughts of newfound pleasures to look at him. Her eyes closed, she tensed, feeling him rubbing himself against her soft opening. It was an odd mix of scalding heat and unyielding hardness. It felt so wicked, so wrong, yet incredibly right. She'd never wanted something as much as she wanted him to touch her, to make her wicked too.

Slowly, Harrison pressed forward, breaking her tight sheath to his larger body. She gasped in surprise to feel him inside, gliding persistently forward, filling her up. She never imagined he would do that. She never imagined it would feel so... so delightful. She gasped, trying to sense past the uncomfortable ache. Harrison licked her neck and she shivered. His hands were on her body, moving smoothly over the sweat that beaded from his deep possession. He rocked in shallow thrusts, massaging her tight passage open, adjusting her slowly to his size.

"Ah," she moaned, her eyes wide.

He rose on his elbow, staring passionately down at her with a look on his face she couldn't comprehend— pain, pleasure, gut-wrenching agony? She shivered to see the pure rawness of his unrefined emotions. She worked her hands over his arms to his neck, rubbing along his face until he turned to nip lightly at her wrist, kissing her racing pulse. She pulled his mouth down to kiss her.

Harrison bit her lips gently, distracting her as he thrust fully within, past the seal of her innocence. He swallowed her gasp of surprise into his mouth, licking tenderly at her lips and teeth as she recovered from the initial shock of his complete entry.

A soft moan sounded in the back of her throat. The pain was only a small annoyance after the pitch his hands, mouth, and eyes had raised her to. She squirmed beneath him. Her knees tightened along his waist, only to release him.

"My lord," she breathed into his soft kiss, moaning and panting, beyond all logical thought or reason. He pulled back, his gaze searching hers in the dim moon- light. His hips moved, his body thrusting gently within her, stroking shallow and deep, rocking against her core as she further adjusted to him. She relaxed to allow him easier entrance.

Harrison groaned, feeling how hot, how tight, how wet, her passage was for him. He pressed deeper still, until he was almost buried to the hilt of his shaft. It was bittersweet agony, holding himself back, rocking in slow thrusts. He couldn't take it. The slickness of her body coated him in acceptance and he knew he had to feel all of her. With a low moan, he gave her his entire thick length, seating himself so that his hips were flush against hers. She whimpered softly but didn't fight the depth as he pulled and thrust himself inside her.

Never could Harrison imagine so much pleasure in one simple act of lovemaking. His heart beat hard in his chest. He loved her, wanted her for so long and now she was his—completely. The thought drove him to madness and he withdrew almost entirely only to thrust again and again.

Elizabeth felt the friction of him building inside her, pushing at her. She saw his muscular form, outlined by blue moonlight, flexing as he moved. She cried out, not caring who heard her. Harrison's mouth pressed to hers, stealing her breath until all she could do was moan lightly into him.

Tension built where he touched. It was almost more than she could bear. She tried to move, tried to learn his rhythm as she worked her hips against him. Her fingers gripped his skin, digging her nails into his hard flesh as she quaked uncontrollably. Her heart hammered so loud she heard it thundering in her ears.

Harrison felt her body coming close to her release. His hips pumped faster, hitting firm and hard against her deep core, pushing her over the edge. Anticipating her scream, he captured her mouth tightly to his as she exploded. His deep kiss muffled her cry as he groaned his release. Tremors shook violently through her, spurring him to bury himself hard and so deep he was sure he touched her very soul. Harrison didn't bother to pull out, knowing that she could never belong to anyone but him as he released himself inside her.

Elizabeth's scream turned to a moan which turned into a soft pant which faded into an incoherent whimper of approval and delight. Her arms fell weakly from him to the bed, nestling into her long hair.

His heart lodged in his throat, Harrison leaned over to kiss her, tender and soft. He'd been with a lot of women but none compared to her—none were so sweet, or so real in their passion. She trembled, quivering where he was still embedded inside her. Reluctant to leave the warmth of her, he forced himself to pull out.

Elizabeth felt her body slowly coming back to reality. Every inch of her tingled with newly discovered pleasures. Feeling the earl's hand on her stomach, caressing lightly, she shivered. She was almost too afraid to look at him.

"Are you cold?" he asked, leaning over to her temple to drop kisses along her hairline.

Harrison rested on his side, facing her. Never had he been so happy. He nibbled along the rim of her ear, wanting instantly to claim her again and again. He couldn't get enough of her taste, her feel.

Instead of answering, for her body felt as if it were still on fire, she opened her eyes to study him. "How many women have you had like this? I know it has to be a great many. Your reputation precedes you."

Harrison nearly choked on his tongue. How could he answer a question like that? Surely the truth would only upset her. Well, at least one form of the truth would. Instead of giving her a number, he thought of the last year spent pining for her and answered cautiously, "None that matter since I first saw you."

Elizabeth forced a small, indifferent chuckle and wondered at his vague answer. They hadn't known each other long. She knew the knowledge shouldn't have bothered her but it did. She didn't want to think of him with anyone else—especially at this moment when he touched her so tenderly, intimately.

"It doesn't matter, mind you," she answered, covering her mouth to yawn. Her face turned away and the long line of her neck strained before his lips.

Harrison couldn't resist. He kissed her throat, licking playfully at it. Her words stung him profoundly but he would never show it. His vanity could convince himself that she was nervous, having lost her virginity to someone who didn't make promises to her.

"How are you?" he asked, again nuzzling her ear. He trailed his hand lower over her hip, rubbing gently. "Sore?"

Elizabeth tried to hide her face at the forward question. "Ah, I... a little."

Harrison chuckled.

Suddenly, she sat up. Glancing around, she tried to avoid looking at his naked body.

"Where...?" he began, reaching to stop her as she hopped off the bed.

"I should get back to my own room." Spying her nightgown, she grabbed it and pulled it over her head.

Harrison threw his legs over the side of the bed to go after her. She was loosely dressed by the time he got there. Wrapping his arms around her waist from behind, he pulled her to his chest, letting her feel the hard length of his desire for her.

"I don't want you to go," he murmured to her neck, loving the way she shivered when he touched her there.

"I can't stay, my lord," she said, trying to shake loose. "I might fall asleep. What if one of the servants comes in and catches us? What would Thomas say?"

"We both know what Thomas would say," said the earl, holding tighter the more she fought to be free. The thick nightgown only added to the softness of her. "He would demand I honor you with marriage."

"Exactly," she breathed, going very still—too still. "Neither of us wants that."

Harrison's breathing deepened as he thought of her words. He wanted it—more than anything, he wanted it. His tone guarded, he asked, "Would being my wife be so bad?"

"Oh," she fumed, turning in his arms to face him. Her brow furrowed with a deep frown. "You can't be serious for a moment, can you? You, my lord rogue, have no desire for a wife. Just as I have no desire for you as a husband. This is an adventure and—"

Harrison kissed her to get her to shut up. He didn't want to listen to her. She felt something for him—something strong enough to make her want to come to him like this.

"If you married me," he said into her lips when his kiss had begun to soften them, "we could make love whenever and however we wanted without fear of being caught."

His hands roamed her gown, grasping at her hair as he deepened his kiss.

Elizabeth hit his shoulder but gasped at the way his tongue darted in and out of her lips, teasing her. She shivered, moaning. The idea suddenly had some merit.

A loud knock on the door stopped them. Elizabeth tensed, pulling back, her eyes wide in fright.

"Harry?" Thomas called. "Are you awake? Can we come in?"

"Hide," Harrison said quietly, pointing to the side of the bed. Elizabeth didn't need to be told twice. She dove to the side of the bed, trying to inch herself beneath the wooden frame. It was a tight fit.

Harrison made sure she was hidden before crossing over to the door. He was naked, so only leaned over enough to peak through the crack. Seeing Thomas and Mr. Turner waiting for him, he forced a sleepy yawn.

Mr. Turner was a studious man who looked more like a banker than an artist. His harsh lips pressed tightly together in a way that made him look like an intolerable bore. However, he was anything but.

"What is it?" the earl asked, blinking as if he just awoke. He made a great show of rubbing his eyes.

"Oh," Thomas mused, shaking his head and laughing. "I forgot it was so late. I wanted to show Mr. Turner that portrait I did of Elizabeth. We were discussing the ability of art to mimic life and I had to tell him of it. Naturally, he wanted to see it for himself."

"I don't have it," the earl lied.

Thomas blinked, an expression between hurt and confusion.

"I sent it on to my estate this morning while you were in your study. I couldn't bear to look at it. It was too disheartening."

"Oh," Thomas said, believing to understand. He delicately waved his hand in disappointment. "I'm sorry to have awakened you."

"Good evening, gentlemen," the earl said. He shut the door. Standing, he breathed deeply. He didn't care for Thomas to discover his sister in his room, not without making an honorable request for her hand first. And he didn't want to have to explain why the portrait was changed—at least not yet.

When he turned around, Elizabeth stood by the edge of the bed and glared at him.

"You have my portrait?" she demanded in anger. She tried to dart to the side, making a move to go around his naked body. Harrison stepped in her way.

"Thomas gave it to me," he answered, not bothering to cover his nakedness.

A lazy smile found its way to his features. He looked her over, prompting her gaze to dip over him. She began to warm, seeing his arousal growing before his flat, hard stomach.

"Oh," she huffed, realizing he distracted her with his steamy looks. "Why would he give it to you? I want it destroyed."

"I wanted it," the earl stated simply. He made a move to go to her. She artfully stepped around him to the door. "And he knew you didn't want it around."

"Well, I didn't want you to have it. Of all people," she growled, irritated. That's not how she wanted him to remember her. That's not how she wanted him to see her. She wanted him to remember her as adventurous and wild as surely no one else would.

"You can't leave yet," he said, his voice quiet.

"You don't own me," Elizabeth said, reaching for the handle. "I can do what I wish."

"Thomas may be out in the hall," he warned. She stiffened and dropped her hand. Harrison came up behind her, reaching around to grab her stomach. He pressed her soft body back into him. Instantly, his lips were on her neck, weakening her resolve to leave.

"Will you check?" she asked, breathless. He cupped her breasts, kneading them, making the tips hard and achy.

"No, I want you to stay. I want to make love to you again and again," Harrison said. He grabbed her shoulders and swung her around to face him. Elizabeth, remembering he had her portrait, struck at his shoulder lightly in defiance. "I want to show you things—such wondrous things that we can do together."

"Get in the bed." Her eyes dipped.

Harrison pulled back to look at her. He grinned, turning to do as she bid.

Elizabeth let her gaze roam freely over his naked backside as longing shot through her. Then, when he crawled onto the mattress, she turned, pulled open the door and ran down the hall, not looking back.

Harrison's smile fell as he turned to find an open door and no Elizabeth. On instinct, he jumped up and ran after her. He was too late. All he saw was the tail end of her nightgown as she rounded a corner. Knowing he couldn't very well go chasing after her naked, he had to let her go.

Elizabeth shut her bedroom door as quietly as she could in her haste. Her heart beat heavily in her chest. Her lungs gasped for air. What did she do? Was she insane going to a rogue's bedroom late at night? But, oh, it had felt so good to be touched by him. His hands, his lips, his delicious body—all could easily melt her. She hurt deep inside where he'd touched her but, strangely, she wanted him to do it again.

Rushing to the mirror, she looked to see if she was changed. Her features were flushed. Her hair was a wild mess around her shoulders. Then, leaning forward in the soft glow of the gas lamp, she pulled her nightgown to the side. There, on her chest, was a mark where the earl's lips had sucked too long and hard. She shivered thinking about it, touching it lightly, secretly liking that she had it. Briefly, she wondered if it would always be there, like a birthmark or if it would go away with time like a bruise.

Elizabeth lay down on her bed, snuggling beneath the covers. Turning to look at her bedroom door, part of her wished the naked earl would come barging through demanding that she make love to him again and again like he had said. Then, remembering what he said about being with other women recently, she frowned.

Hardening herself to him, she turned her back on the door. He was merely an adventure, nothing more. And, surely, what they did together had nothing to do with love.

Harrison went over to the portrait in disappointment, swinging the blanket off it. He gasped to see a small glimmer of light had been added to its painted eyes. They seemed almost playful. He swallowed, staring into them as he fell to his knees to kneel naked before it. He didn't know what exactly had sent Elizabeth away from him but he would find out.

He could still feel her on his body, taste her on his mouth. He lifted his hand to caress the paint, only to fall back without meeting the canvas. Moaning, he closed his eyes and shook his head. "Tell me portrait, what other adventures shall I give to her? What will make her happy? What will make her fall for me as I have her?"

Slowly, he opened his eyes. Almost instantly, he saw

a gun in her hands, pointed down. He gasped, pulling away in fright.

"What is this?" he asked, almost anxious. "She wishes for my death?"

The painting seemed to quiver in the moonlight, rippling with a life of its own. Harrison blinked, in a daze. Nothing changed on the surface. The gun was very real and in her hands. He forced his heart to slow from the initial shock.

"Surely if she wanted me dead, the gun would be pointed at me, not down," he reasoned. He pushed himself up to standing. "That's it. I'll teach her how to use a pistol."

13

GETTING ELIZABETH TO TALK TO HIM, LET ALONE listen to him proved harder than Harrison could've realized. The next morning, he found her in the dining room, speaking to her brother and Mr. Turner. Neither man looked as if they had been to bed the night before. They contrasted greatly to the reserved, rested beauty at their side.

Elizabeth wore a very proper gown of pale yellow and cream. The bodice pulled high on her chest to hide her very soft breasts from his view. All too well he remembered the feel of them. Harrison couldn't help but smile as Elizabeth acknowledged his entrance. But she merely nodded briefly and turned back to her conversation with the others. She didn't deign to speak directly to him.

Harrison's temperament only grew dismal as the meal went on. Not once did Elizabeth look at him. When he asked her a polite question, her words were curt and to the point. In fact, to the earl's jealousy, she showed the studious Mr. Turner too much flattering attention. So much consideration that even Thomas took note of her interest in the man. He directed a brief look of pity on the earl, before rejoining Elizabeth and Mr. Turner's conversation once more.

After breakfast, Elizabeth excused herself. She nodded briefly at the three men, who rose as she stood from the table. Then, taking her leave, she strode from the dining room.

Harrison watched after her with heated eyes. Then, turning to Thomas, he said, "If you gentlemen would excuse me."

Thomas waved him away. When he was gone, Mr. Turner turned to the viscount, and said, "Tell me Caldwell, has he asked for your sister's hand yet? I daresay with the way the earl looks at her it won't be long."

"No but I have no doubt he will eventually," Thomas answered, not surprised by his astute friend's assessment.

"But I must wonder why," Mr. Turner mused. "She hardly seems his brand of woman, no offense to your lovely sister."

"None taken," Thomas chuckled.

"And she hardly seems to return his affections," Mr. Turner finished.

"Ah, perhaps that's the attraction," Thomas answered. "We always want what we can't have."

"No," Mr. Turner denied with a small, thoughtful smile. "Not always."

"Elizabeth!" the earl yelled, chasing after her.

Elizabeth stiffened and she looked around the front hall to make sure they were alone before facing him. Her gaze hard, eyed him in dispassion.

"Oh," she grumbled, keeping her voice down. She swatted her hands frantically in his direction. "Do go away. Not now."

"What?" Harrison asked. A frown marred his brow.

"I know you've come to tease me," she said. "I'm in no mood for it, my lord. Go away. Quick, before you're seen talking to me."

Elizabeth tried to walk away from him. He grabbed her elbow, stopping her. She blinked in surprise that he would dare so much in the front hall. She jerked her arm away. Harrison grinned sheepishly.

"Come with me," he urged, trying his best to ignore

her ill-humor. Maybe she was insecure. It was doubtful by the irritated look on her face but he could still hope.

"Where?" she asked, suspicious.

"I want to take you on another adventure," he said, his lids dipping leisurely over his handsome eyes.

Elizabeth looked him over as if seeing his cream waistcoat for the first time that morning when in actuality she hadn't seen anything but him since he walked into the dining room. Oh but he made a fine figure to look at. The linen of his shirt rose above his knotted tie, though the knot was loose with his usual carelessness. His hair appeared slightly damp, though it was drying in fantastically devilish waves.

"What? Now?" she inquired, surprised. She again took him in, her eyes journeying with a feminine interest she didn't realize she should hide from him.

Harrison grinned at her assumption. His voice lowered with meaning as his gaze leisurely moved over her neck and chest. "That's not what I had in mind, Miss Elizabeth. But, if you insist, I can change my plans."

He reached forward to touch her chest hidden beneath the pale yellow. Elizabeth froze, waiting for it. Her eyes rounded.

The dining room door flung open before he ever reached her. Harrison took an automatic step back. To

Elizabeth's dismay, he announced loudly, "Well, here is your brother now. Let us ask his permission."

Elizabeth's jaw dropped slightly at the earl's audacity, though she was partly excited by it, too. She hated to admit his bold confidence attracted her on many levels.

"What's this?" Thomas asked, pausing in his theological debate with Mr. Turner to look at his sister.

"I—" Elizabeth began, ready to denounce the earl as a fool.

"I was going to take Miss Elizabeth out to shoot a pistol. It's a bit unrefined but I believe her reputation will recover," the earl said, smiling widely.

Thomas blinked at the request, leaning over to study Elizabeth who quickly came around the earl's back to study him. To her own surprise, she said, "Yes, Thomas, do let me learn. With all those... indelicacies on the road to London as of late, I should like to be able to defend myself."

Mr. Turner nodded thoughtfully, turning to Thomas. "Yes, Caldwell. It's quite terrible. Some of our fine ladies feel trapped indoors with that scoundrel of a thief on the loose. I remember reading something of it in the paper."

"I see no real harm in it," Thomas answered at last. "Turner and I have to go over some more of my paintings so we can't join you. But, please, feel free to use my dueling pistols in the library. They were father's and a bit old but they should work fine. I believe there is some gun powder around here somewhere. Mayhap one of the servants would know. They are sure to know where I keep everything."

As soon as Thomas and his friend left, Elizabeth frowned and moved to study the earl. "What are you up to, my lord?"

"I want you to come out shooting with me," Harrison said.

His gaze turned so innocent that she knew the look was a lie. Her body shivered, remembering all too well the feel of him. She was still angry at him for taking her portrait and not telling her about it. Before she could respond, he turned away from her, striding into Thomas' study to gather the pistols.

Elizabeth shook her head, trying to pretend she was more vexed than thrilled. But, shooting her father's pistols was always something she dreamt of trying. She couldn't hide her excitement in the plan for long—even if she were going to do it in the company of the all too roguish earl.

14

Elizabeth grabbed the flintlock pistol with both hands, feeling the heavy weight of it in her fingers. A slow smile crept to her features and she bit the corner of her lip to hold it down. Harrison watched her, enthralled beyond words by the joyful look she tried to conceal from him.

"Now, cock back the hammer like I showed you," the earl instructed. He dropped his voice to a whisper, using his instructions as an excuse to come near her. They were close to the house, in the side field. Harrison had the servants set up targets stuffed with hay. Letting his breath hit delicately on the back of her sensitive neck, he said, "Now aim."

Elizabeth shut her eyes as the target blurred before her vision. The earl's nearness was doing wicked things to her self-control. His breath whispered along her nape. She loved it when he'd caressed the back of her neck with his lips. It gave her goosebumps thinking about it. Her whole body tingled with memories of his touch. She shivered again.

"I won't hit anyone walking by, will I?" she asked, considering the far-off horizon line.

The earl chuckled. The shot wouldn't reach a quarter of that distance. His low voice rumbled over her shoulder as he answered, "No."

Elizabeth nearly swooned, only at the last minute remembering to catch herself. Pretending to hate him got harder by the minute until she barely remembered why she even tried. Was it such a big deal he had her portrait, anyway?

"Fire when ready," he instructed. Her shoulder trembled as the pistol dipped lightly to the ground only to pull back up. He stepped back.

Elizabeth aimed and squeezed the trigger. The gun went off with a light cloud of smoke, jolting her arms. Elizabeth gasped in instant pleasure. Grinning widely, she exclaimed, "Oh! Did you see that?"

The earl merely grinned. She looked at him, reluctant to hand him back the pistol as she gripped it in her fingers.

"Did I hit it?" Elizabeth beamed happily.

"I believe you nicked the corner. Not bad for your first time."

When he held out his hand for the pistol so he could reload, she finally released it. Her smile faded and she pretended not to care for his compliment.

"It seems you do many things well your first time," he said.

It took Elizabeth a minute, but she finally got his meaning. Her cheeks paled and her eyes rounded in horror. "How dare you mention such a thing to me?"

Harrison grinned. Her eyes darted around as if they were being watched. The servants in the house couldn't hear a thing. Thomas and Mr. Turner would be confined with the paintings and there weren't any windows in the studio showing the side field.

"Why do you insist on taunting me?" she grumbled, seeing his impossible look.

"Why do you insist on ignoring me in front of your brother?" Harrison asked. His tone was light as was the expression on his face but Elizabeth felt a chill to his clipped words. He busied himself with the gun, refusing to look at her directly.

"We have been through this, my lord. Ours is a *private* arrangement. I shouldn't care if we are strangers in public."

The earl flinched. That hurt him deeply. He felt

used. Instead of laying voice to his injury, he said, daring a glance into her eyes, "I know you like me a little. Admit it."

"I'll admit," she began carefully, studying him. She tried not to let her heart flutter in her chest. He was too handsome. She wished he had some defect to his features. Maybe then he wouldn't occupy so many of her thoughts. "You're diverting."

"Ah," Harrison laughed. He handed the loaded pistol back to her. He let his hand run over her wrist as she took it. To his delight, she shivered at his touch. "It's not a declaration of affection but I'll gladly take it. At least you're no longer accusing me of overstaying my welcome."

"It did no good to remind you of the fact, my lord, so why bother repeating myself?" Elizabeth countered, quite serious when she looked him over.

"I thought you liked to hear yourself speak," Harrison said with great flair. "Please, if it makes you happy to denounce me, then by all means, denounce."

Elizabeth dropped her arms. "Can't you ever be serious?"

"Why?" he murmured, letting his gaze dip to her full lips. "You're serious enough for the both of us."

"Oh, you're incorrigible," she said, cocking back the

hammer and aiming at the target. For a moment, she thought about aiming it at him.

"Thank you, Miss Elizabeth." He came to stand too close behind her. She could feel the heat from his body.

"It wasn't a compliment," she said wryly.

"And, yet, I shall take it as such." Looking at the lowering weapon, he commanded, "Take your shot."

"However did you become friends with Thomas?" Elizabeth stepped closer to the target to get away from him. She pulled the trigger, firing. She again jumped in excitement as the smoke cleared. Lowering the weapon, she handed it over to the earl's awaiting hands. "No doubt he keeps you around merely as an artistic amusement."

"However did *you* become a sibling to Thomas?" the earl countered. "I don't see how you could've sprung from the same—"

"Really, my lord." she broke in to stop his words. "The things you say."

"What?" he shrugged, unaffected by her scolding. "You wish for me to be silent?"

"I don't think it possible for you not to speak. I have tried to quiet you on many occasions without success."

"There is one way to silence my tongue." Harrison grinned, his dimple peeking out at her.

"Pray tell," she said matter-of-factly in her obvious doubt.

"You can kiss me again," he announced. His gaze dipped over her waist. "Or let me kiss you."

"Oh. You promised never to breathe a word of that!" She turned, although the prospect of another kiss wasn't all that unwelcome.

"I promised not to tell anyone else about kissing you. You already know about it," he answered. Coming near her back, he lifted his arm by her side and aimed using one hand. Elizabeth gasped, darting around him. He waited until she was safely behind his back before firing. The shot was dead on. "What do you say? Would you like another secret to write about in your diary?"

"I don't keep a diary," she answered, awed by his skill.

"Well, now you can," he laughed. "You'll have something to put in it."

"Really, how you do go on," she scolded.

"You wouldn't let me go on, though I tried." He looked at her, piercing her with meaning.

Elizabeth suddenly felt very vulnerable. "I don't understand you. Now, be quiet and reload. It's my turn."

Harrison obeyed, reloading in silence. When she aimed to pistol and cocked the hammer back, he leaned close to her ear and asked, "Do you want me to make love to you again? Right now? Right here? I can barely contain myself. Who cares if the servants see us?"

Elizabeth gasped. The pistol shot wildly to the right, missing the target altogether. Strange sensations threatened her sanity. With a huff, she faced him. Her mouth opened but no sound came out. She shoved the pistol into his chest, giving it back to him.

"*Argh.*" She grumbled under her breath, stalking away without a backward glance.

Harrison watched her leave, a small smile on his face. Grabbing the pistols and their supplies, he moved to follow her. She was already to the side gardens when he caught up to her. Setting the pistols down on a table near the house, he said, "Elizabeth, wait."

Elizabeth jolted at his voice but didn't stop walking. She quickened her pace, disappearing around a shrub.

"Elizabeth!" He frowned, following her. "Stop!"

Harrison jogged once he was out of eyesight of the house. Grabbing her arm, he pulled it firmly.

"Please, stop," he said. "What's wrong?"

"You're so... impossible sometimes," she countered heatedly. "Why must you mock me at every turn?"

"Mock you?" he shot in surprise.

"Yes, mock me. I can't help that I'm not as experienced as you... when it comes to... controlling my urges but it doesn't mean you need to throw them in my face."

Elizabeth tried to leave him, intent on running away in her mortification. Harrison stopped her.

"What are you talking about?" he asked.

"Oh, like it's not obvious," she fumed. "You know I'm attracted to you and surely you know the effect your nearness has on women."

"Are you saying I have an effect on you?" His voice was quiet. He dared not hope.

"You very well know you do. But, must you mention it at every turn and taunt me with it? At the very least you could act like a gentleman and pretend as if nothing happened."

"Why should I pretend? When we both know something has happened? It's not like I'm declaring our actions to the world."

"To... be polite," she answered.

"Would that please you?" Harrison's voice dipped and his face hardened. Elizabeth looked at him, her brow furrowed. "Is that how you would have me behave? Do you want me to be a perfect gentleman, proper, refined, boring? Would that please you, Elizabeth? For say the word and I'll never taunt you again."

"Yes... no, I don't know." Elizabeth reached to pluck absently at a nearby leaf. "I'm not asking you to change for I haven't that right to do so. I don't want you having fun at my expense, my lord. I know you have no true feelings for me." She stopped, glancing at him for confirmation. He said nothing and she hastened, "And I'm perfectly fine with that. But you don't have to throw my... sudden wantonness in my face at every turn."

"What are you speaking of?" Harrison frowned, not following her rush of logic.

"When you said you wanted to... in front of the servants," she said. Her eyes filled with moisture and she blinked it back. "I know it's obvious that I wanted... and you obviously only wanted to tease. Oh, you're insufferable. I don't like you at all. I don't know why I bother."

A wide grin spread over Harrison's features dimpling his cheek. She was mad because she desired him and thought he mocked her for it. Was she so foolish not to know he'd spent the entire morning mad with lust for her? That even now his body was erect from watching the movements of her lips as she spoke? Looking at her face, he realized she hadn't known he teased her because he wanted her. He was amazed at how a woman so passionate could also be such an innocent.

"I wish you'd leave here and never come back," Elizabeth said in response to his handsome devil-may-care smile, "at least until I'm married and living elsewhere."

His smiled faded, leaving his face hard. "You dare to mention marrying another man in front of me?"

Elizabeth stiffened at the anger in his low words. She

took a step back. His possessive gaze sent a thrill through her. "Well, I assume I'll marry someday, my lord. It should be no secret. All women must marry. It's what is expected."

"I thought you were beyond living by society's rules." His tone didn't lighten.

"In private, yes," she answered, "but in public I must keep up appearances. We have agreed on this. In fact, those were your words not mine, though I do quite agree with them. Are you worried that I'll forget that you're my friend? Is that why you're angry?"

Harrison didn't move, barely breathed.

"Unless I marry for love," Elizabeth said, stepping up to touch his jacket. Oh but he was handsome. She doubted she would ever have her fill of him. She knew her next words would be sinfully wicked but she couldn't stop them. "Unless I love my husband, I should say there is no reason why we both can't continue our private friendship if that's what we both wish at the time. More discretion will obviously have to be taken under such circumstances but it could be a grand adventure. In public, we won't have to speak at all. In fact, we can ignore each other. Thomas won't even know of it. No one will suspect us and if aught is ever said. The gossipmongers will be laughed at because the notion will appear far too silly to believe."

"And what if I love my wife?" he asked.

Elizabeth wondered at the harshness of his voice but couldn't help laughing at him. "Oh, my lord. We both know you will never love a woman in such a way. It's one of the reasons I'm drawn to you, I think. Because I know you will never come to care for me above our friendship and so neither of us risks our heart in this venture. We can have the fun without the involvement of emotions."

Harrison still didn't move, didn't try to deny her words. Elizabeth's heart fell slightly in her chest and an ache formed in the hollow it left in its wake. For some insane reason she couldn't name, she waited for him to deny her charge. He didn't and she knew it was for the best. It wasn't like anything more could come of them than they already shared.

"Besides, the idea of you married is absurd in and of itself," she rambled. "I do suppose a proper match will be made for you eventually, for the sake of your title and family line. But, you? Marry for love? No, if you have your choice of a bride, I can only imagine you will choose her for the prettiness of her face. And still, I doubt that will content you—not a man of your reputation and appetites. If not with me, I do see you having many affairs."

Still silence from him.

"Let us not speak of this anymore, Lord Wrotham,"

Elizabeth said asserting a boldness she didn't feel inside. His eyes bore forward with an unnatural seriousness as she spoke. The subject pained her greatly and she didn't wish to delve into why. "We have no real future together and there is no reason I can foresee in planning one. Besides, the grandness of our venture is that it is what it is. It may end tomorrow or when we are fifty. Let us enjoy it either way and have no regrets when it's finished."

Harrison stepped to her and pulled her hard into him. His chest rose and fell with heavy breaths. He thrust his erection into her hard and rubbed it along her stomach, causing her to gasp. "So, this is all you want from me?"

"Yes," she lied, staring at his neck. "It's all I'm asking —for however long we both wish it."

"You wish me to pleasure you?" His mouth moved closer to her temple.

"Yes, please, yes," she sighed. Her lids fluttered shut. She panted in longing. "And I want you to teach me how to pleasure you. I want to touch you. I want you to show me everything you know."

"Everything?" he chuckled to himself.

Harrison held her, letting her feel him. It was a bittersweet ache that formed in his chest. She admitted to wanting him, which was something in and of itself.

But she also admitted to never seeing herself as having feelings for him. She wanted him as her lover—her plaything. It was a vicious bite into his soul, his heart. He would be everything to her as she was to him. Did he take what she offered or did he demand more from her? In demanding her heart, he knew he could very well lose all of her. It wasn't a risk he was willing to take. He was a starved man and he would take whatever she could, *would* give him. His only hope was that in time, she would retract her words and realize she loved him.

Elizabeth, unaware of the turmoil in him, nodded. Her lips parted in hopes he would steal one kiss. She loved the feel of his mouth on hers—on her body.

"Then my first lesson, Elizabeth, will be that anticipation makes passion all the more enjoyable." Harrison swallowed, wanting nothing more than to kiss her until she gasped his name. But he needed to think, to strategize. He needed to ask the damned portrait how to win her heart, her soul, her very being.

To her amazement, Harrison let her go, turned, and left her standing alone in the garden. She watched him leave, wondering at the cold look he shot her before rounding the corner.

Elizabeth felt like he'd kicked her in the gut. Her body ached with need for him and she could barely think beyond it. Weakly, she turned, walking in the opposite direction into the gardens. She couldn't face him, not now. Not with a rejection like that looming over her. How could he dismiss her so easily as if she didn't affect him? Numb, she walked faster, refusing to cry.

Harrison growled to himself. He stopped, looking back to the shrubs that hid her from view. He turned to her, only to stop and try to leave her. Looking down his body, he groaned. It was no use. He couldn't deny himself when she was so willing. Cursing himself as weak, he moved to go back to her. When he came around the corner, she was gone.

ELIZABETH RAN DOWN THE EARTHEN PATH, TO THE farthest reaches of the garden. Stopping at a secluded alcove, she stood, staring into the shadowed hollow. She panted from the sprint and a thin sheen of perspiration dotted her skin.

She stepped into the shadows when she felt a hand on her arm. Harrison's voice drifted over her, saying, "Second lesson, surprises are even sweeter than anticipation."

A shiver ran over her body at his husky tone. He ran his hands down her arms, warm and caressing. He took a step forward, forcing her into the shadowy alcove.

When they were hidden from the garden paths, he said, "Turn to me."

Elizabeth readily obeyed. She looked at him, trusting. Her gaze was a bit moist, but she blinked the tears away before they could fall.

"Unfasten my breeches," he murmured, a light smile curling on the side of his mouth. His eyes bore into her and she shivered. He dropped his hands to his sides and didn't move.

Elizabeth's fingers trembled as she undid his breeches. When they were loose about his hips, he walked past her and came to sit on a stone bench.

"Come here, Elizabeth," Harrison said. "Kneel before me."

Elizabeth obeyed, adjusting her skirts as she did so. Her heart beat furiously in her chest. His face gave nothing away but she could see the pulse racing along his neck. He was excited as she. His game thrilled her and she found herself anticipating more orders.

"Take me from my breeches," he murmured, watching her. His knees parted to allow her body to fit between them. He leaned back, stretching his arms over the bench's top. "Take out my arousal. I want you to touch it."

Elizabeth worked out the smooth, hard length of him, pulling his breeches open to expose not only his rigid shaft but the two softer globes beneath. Veins pulsed along the sides of it. The size of him thrilled her, made her hot for him. She tried to stand, but he shot forward, holding her where she was.

"But...?" Elizabeth looked helplessly at his arousal. "I'm ready. I want to... us to..."

"Who is the instructor here?"

"You," she said, a small smile coming unbidden to her lips.

"And do you still want me to teach you how to pleasure me?"

Elizabeth nodded.

"Then open your mouth. Wet your lips for me," he urged, his eyes darkening. His hand left her shoulder and again returned to lie across the back of the bench. Elizabeth obeyed, watching his face for approval. Harrison groaned. "Now, wet the tip of my arousal. Lick at it with your tongue, taste it."

Elizabeth swallowed and leaned forward, her tongue darting out to taste his smooth tip. His stomach tensed when she touched him. His thighs tightened along her sides and she gripped them for support. A low moan came from him.

The light darts of her tongue drove him mad. She glided her hands up his thighs, edging closer with tormenting slowness.

"Harder," he groaned. "Lick me harder."

Elizabeth obliged, pressing her tongue fully to him.

She ran it up the shaft. A bead of moisture came from the tip. Without stopping to think, she ran her tongue over it and tasted his essence. A light hum left her throat.

Harrison jerked. He took her hands, moving one to cup the soft globes beneath his shaft, the other to wrap around the root of his erection. He drew her hand, teaching her to squeeze and move over him. Elizabeth kept licking him, tasting him, rubbing and stroking him. As her lips parted, he jerked his hips up past her teeth.

"In your mouth," he grunted. He stroked the top of her hair, playing in the soft tendrils that had come loose. "Suck me."

Elizabeth obeyed. How could she not? When his voice strained, commanding, begging, wanting. Her lips parted, sucking along his flesh, loving the power she had over him, loving the low grunts of masculine approval he made in the back of his throat.

"Enough," he gasped, pulling her off him. She was reluctant to let go. Before she could speak, he said, his voice hoarse, "Come here."

Harrison helped to lift her skirts and pulled her forward to straddle his body. The warm spring air drifted around them, scented with flowers and fresh country air. Birds sang quiet songs in the distance.

Elizabeth chuckled as he fought her petticoats. He dug his hands until he found the flesh of her hips. He brought his fingers to her, testing and teasing her as he discovered her wetness. Finding her body hot and ready, he moaned.

"We should have found a better place to play," he murmured, burying his face into her chest.

"What's wrong with here?"

"I would have you again in the comfort of my bed," he answered. He drew his kisses along her skin. His body was brought to a feverish pitch by the workings of her soft lips. He tried to slow, to calm himself.

"Is there a reason you wait, my lord?" she whimpered. She smiled shyly at him. She stroked his handsome face. "For I think the anticipation will surely kill me."

He chuckled. Lifting her, he drew her body to his. His hard male flesh brushed against her and she shivered.

Elizabeth's lips trembled violently and she sucked in a deep breath. Her body tensed, waiting for that first jab of pain before the pleasure. Harrison groaned, pulling her down hard against him. Her body stretched, taking him in. There was soreness deep inside but nothing like the night before.

"What are you doing?"

"Ah," Elizabeth frowned, pushing down on him. "You're not hurting me. I thought that..."

Elizabeth blushed, unable to continue.

Harrison balked in disbelief. "It only hurts that once. Now come and kiss me. I want to feel your lips."

Elizabeth smiled, pressing her mouth to his. She kissed him deeply as his hands lifted her, showing her how to ride him. Her body took him in, gliding over him in deep, slow strokes. She moaned as the friction built.

"I want more." She gripped his shoulders.

"Then take it." Harrison let her hips go, amazed when she began lifting on him, following his direction but taking it faster and harder. "*Elizabeth.*"

She became encouraged by the almost painful, guttural way he groaned her name. She liked his voice, liked how it washed over her, adding to her pleasure. She discovered her passion for him, trying different rhythms until she found the right one that sent her hips rocking hard into him. His shaft hit her deep, pushing and rubbing in a way that drove her over the edge.

"Ah, Elizabeth, kiss me now," he ordered. "Scream into my mouth."

She whimpered. The sound of her noisy climax was on the edge of her tongue, ready to be released along with her body. His hand shot up, forcing her lips to his just as the tremors hit her in shuddering waves. A loud moan left her lips and he captured it inside him, swallowing it up so she wouldn't be overheard.

Harrison smothered his lips to hers, cutting off her breath as her tight passage clenched him. He exploded into her. He gave all of himself to her, not concerned about the consequences. He wanted her. He needed her. And, so help him, he was going to make her love him. Like it or not, she was his—forever.

Now, all he had to do was convince her of it.

Harrison released her lips. Their heavy breaths mingled hot and ragged, echoing in the alcove. Elizabeth's fingers still gripped his face, holding him close. Slowly, she let him go. She dug her fingers into his jacket.

"Is it always like this?" she asked.

"With us it will be," Harrison promised, placing a light kiss to her lips.

"You know what I mean," Elizabeth insisted, still panting and weak.

Harrison did, and he didn't like it. He urged her off him and began righting his clothes. He refused to answer.

"I mean will it be like this with other men?" she asked, wondering why he suddenly frowned at her. She couldn't imagine anyone else making her feel as she did at this moment.

His smile was hard. "You think to go to other men so soon?"

"It's just a question," she defended. "I'm merely curious. Don't look at me like that. It was your suggestion I experience all life has to offer."

"I didn't mean to experience it as a—"

"I dare you to finish that sentence, my lord." Elizabeth glared at him. Harrison's frown deepened. "If I'm anything, it's of your doing. Besides, if I care not for the rules of society, what makes you think your opinion means aught to me? What makes you think you mean aught to me?"

Elizabeth covered her mouth with her hands. Instantly, she shook her head in remorse.

"I... I didn't mean that." She reached for him but he jerked back. Her body was still shaky from his touch.

"Didn't you?"

"No, my lo—"

"Damnation. It's Harrison. Say it, Elizabeth. I think we are a little beyond the formality of titles." Harrison's eyes were tortured when they turned to her. "It's not like we're strangers."

"It's not proper to... someone would suspect us if I called you by your given name." She stared at him and she tried to back away to the entrance of the alcove.

"It's not like anyone will hear you. And are you so ashamed to be with me that you must hide that we are friends?"

"My lord," she began, trying to pacify him with her tone. "Please, don't—"

"I'll take care of this right now," he stated darkly.

Elizabeth's mouth fell open as he tried to storm past her. She grabbed his arm, jerking him with all her strength to keep him back. "Wait. What will you do?"

"I'm going to speak to your brother." Harrison's gaze bore into her, hard.

Elizabeth paled. "You wouldn't dare. What of your friendship with him? He will never forgive this. He will never trust either of us again. Why would you do that? Does he mean so little to you?"

Harrison smiled. He lifted his fingers to touch her cheek. Elizabeth wanted to pull away but she couldn't. There was something in the softening of his expression that held her. "Come to my bed tonight. Come to be with me again."

"What?" she asked. Was he mad? They were fighting. He was threatening to expose them.

"Just come," he said softly. And with those words, he was gone.

Elizabeth didn't know how to act around the earl in front of her brother and Mr. Turner, so she treated him the same as she always had. She had to admit that there was something wickedly enjoyable about slighting him in public, knowing him intimately as she did. Also, she liked sparring verbally with him. It made her blood boil to know he could give as well as she gave in their verbal play and Thomas and Mr. Turner were none the wiser for it.

After dinner, the men retired for cigars and brandy. Elizabeth wished that she could join them but it wasn't proper for a lady to do so. Instead, she was forced to wait until evening. She ordered a bath, taking her time with it, daydreaming about the earl. She hated to admit it but she was worried that she might become too attached to him.

"Don't be silly, Elizabeth," she mumbled to herself. She came from the bathwater and wrapped a linen around her body. "You're thinking that way because he's new to you because what he does to you is so new. If you were to sleep with Mr. Turner, it would be the same as..."

Elizabeth frowned. Thinking of Mr. Turner in such a way brought her no rush of pleasure. In fact, it left her body feeling a little dead. She closed her eyes tight and tried to imagine it. But, every time she tried to imagine Mr. Turner's lips on her breast, the image would melt and suddenly it was Lord Wrotham's gaze looking up at her. She shivered.

Well, surely Mr. Turner was the wrong man to try to prove a point with. It didn't change the fact that the earl was an adventure and nothing more. It's not like they had a future.

"I WISH TO MARRY YOUR SISTER," HARRISON SAID, looking at Thomas' face. Thomas stared absently at the flames, lost in artistic thoughts. Mr. Turner had gone to retrieve a journal filled with notes about the viscount's upcoming art show in London and the earl wanted to speak his mind before the man came back.

"I know, Harry," Thomas said almost sadly. He stared at the flames a while longer, sighing heavily.

"Well?" Harrison demanded, a little harsher than he would've liked.

"Well, what, Harry?" Thomas asked, blinking. He turned to his friend expectantly.

"Do I have your permission or not?"

"Oh," Thomas mumbled. It was clear by his confusion that he tried to follow. He looked blankly at the earl for a long moment before gasping, "Oh! You're asking my permission to marry Elizabeth. My apologies, Harry, I thought you were merely stating the obvious. Forgive me."

Harrison let a small chuckle cross his lips. He did love the absentminded Thomas like he was a brother and readily forgave him for not paying attention three-quarters of the time.

"Well?" Harrison asked at last, thinking the man's thoughts again drifted.

"No, I did not forget you again, Harry," Thomas said quietly. "I was merely thinking of it."

"You have to think of my request? Do you doubt my sincerity?" Harrison asked, a little hurt.

"A year ago, yes, I would have. However, now, I'm not so sure. I can see you love my sister and as her brother and guardian, you can't deny me the right to contemplate your past behavior with women. I'm inclined to think you have changed in that regard. My only concern is will you change back?"

There was no judgment in Thomas' tone, only thoughtful questioning.

"No," Harrison said. "I would swear to you on all I have—my title, my fortune, my life—that I won't stray from her. You know I never give my word without meaning and truth. And I give you my word, on my honor, that, if she were mine, I would care for her better than my own life."

Thomas gave a small smile. "Ah, then it's settled. If she will have you, she's yours. I won't force her hand."

"I wouldn't ask it of you." Harrison let a smile cross his features. He hadn't realized he held his breath, waiting for Thomas' approval. His heart beat, hard, slow, nervous.

"Do you have reason to think that she will have you?" Thomas asked, his eyes doubtful.

"Very little," Harrison admitted. The image of Elizabeth's passion-laden face came to him, of her dark eyes hazy with the pleasure she derived from his body.

"After her treatment of you, I daresay your suit doesn't look promising," Thomas said.

"And yet, I can do nothing else." Harrison's mouth turned down. The brightness of his eyes faded until he was left looking heartbroken and miserable.

Thomas stood. Moving to the decanter of brandy, he poured some for the earl and then himself. Raising his snifter, he said, "The best of luck, Harry, the best of luck."

Harrison nodded, drinking quietly. No more was

said as Mr. Turner came through the door, muttering about a description for one of the paintings. Thomas nodded sadly at the earl before turning his attention back to his work. Lord Wrotham stood, taking his leave and receiving absent waves from the two men as they argued the fine points of art and its role in modern society.

Harrison looked warily at the painting, feeling very tense. The blanket covered the portrait's face and he trembled as he thought of what to ask it. He tried to ask if Elizabeth would say yes to being his wife should he ask her, but the finality of what the portrait would tell him kept the words from leaving his throat. Swallowing nervously he asked, "Tell me portrait, do I have a chance at making Elizabeth my wife, if but a slim one?"

He lifted his fingers to the blanket and he drew it slowly back. The brandy swirled in his stomach, threatening to make him sick. His eyes closed and he took a calming breath before he could look. As his eyes opened, he heard a knock on the door. The blanket slipped from his fingers but not before he saw the smile on Elizabeth's painted face had grown.

His heart skipped. He crossed over to the door, throwing it open, ready to declare his love... to a maid. The woman jolted to see the earl grinning widely at her, his eyes sparkling. A blush came over her features as she shyly looked to the floor.

"My lord," the red-headed servant said, daring a glance up at him. In her hands, she gripped a fresh decanter of dark brandy. "The viscount bid me to bring this to your chambers, my lord."

Harrison tried to hide his disappointment as he waved her in. The maid dutifully curtsied and passed by him. Harrison waited, the door open, for her to finish. His linen shirt hung loosely at his waist, open at the throat. His bare feet stood unmoving on the carpet.

The maid grabbed the chamber's nearly empty decanter and curtsied again as she passed by the earl at the door. Then, turning, she glanced up to him, her eyes shining with an unmistakable invitation.

Harrison looked at her. She was a very beautiful woman, lush lips that rounded and pursed slightly. Her look was one he knew well. She wanted him.

"Is there aught else, my lord?" she asked, her tone dipping. Her arms hugged the bottle to her stomach, artfully thrusting her large breasts up. It was a move to draw his attention. It worked. His eyes dipped down.

"No," Harrison said. A year ago, before seeing Elizabeth, he would've taken her offer. But, now, she held only a passing interest to him.

The maid's face fell in shock that he rejected her offer. She blinked, standing before him in confusion. The maid wet her thick lips. Her lids lowered and she dared a step closer to the earl. Lifting a hand to his shirt, she asked, "Are you quite sure, my lord? I could help you change for the night."

Harrison opened his mouth to respond. His gaze flitted down the hall. Elizabeth stood there, her face stricken. She ducked around the corner. Harrison frowned, knowing what she would assume.

"No," the earl said, stopping the maid from following his gaze down the hall. "That won't be necessary."

The girl's mouth fell slack and she took a hasty step back. Mumbling under her breath, she said, "Very good, my lord."

Harrison waited for her to disappear, before jogging silently down the hall after Elizabeth. To his surprise, he found her hugged to the wall, just around the corner. She looked up, startled.

"My lord," she gasped, breathless and surprised.

"Come on, it's safe, hurry," Harrison went to pull her arm. She avoided his hand and backed away.

"You seem to be busy," she said. "It's fine. Go ahead."

"What?" Harrison frowned at her. He knew well what she suspected. "Nothing happened."

"You don't have to explain it to me," Elizabeth said, her voice rising slightly. "You can do whatever you wish with the maids, so long as they are willing."

"Would you be quiet," he ordered under his breath. He glanced around the hall before moving to look at his bedroom door. Grabbing her hand, he didn't give her a choice as he pulled her to his room. Once he had the door shut behind him, he turned to study her.

"I wasn't coming here," she protested.

"I think you were."

Elizabeth trembled. There was no point in trying to lie. "All right, my lord, I was. But that was before I saw you with the maid."

"Are you jealous?" he asked, his brow arching.

Elizabeth frowned. "Jealous? Me? No. I told you, I care not who or what you do."

"Then why are you shaking?"

"I'm cold," she said, willing her arms to still.

Elizabeth was jealous, insanely so. Her first impulse, after she kept herself from retching, was to tear the maid's hair from her pretty little head.

"Come, let me warm you," he said. He crossed quickly over to her and made a move as if to touch her.

Elizabeth pulled away. She crossed over to the brandy on the dresser. "I think I'll try this instead."

Harrison sighed. "It's brandy. Perhaps, too strong for you."

"You, of all people, think to deny me a whim?" Elizabeth laughed. "I've always wanted to try this and port but mother always said it wasn't ladylike to consume such things."

"She was right," Harrison said, though he knew plenty ladies who did.

"My point exactly," Elizabeth said. She poured a little into a glass and sniffed.

Harrison was hard pressed not to laugh as her nose wrinkled. Wryly, he asked, "Would you like a cigar to go with it?"

Elizabeth smiled and instantly nodded.

"I was teasing, Elizabeth." Harrison again went to her, drawn to be near her. "I don't think it a good idea."

"And I'm not. I do wish to try one," she said. She braved a little sip and coughed. He smirked. Elizabeth lifted her hand to his chest and let it rest, "Please, my lord, let me try one."

Harrison sighed. One look into her eyes and he would give her anything. Crossing over to his jacket, which he'd flung over a chair earlier, he obtained a cigar from the pocket. Then crossing to the large window, he pulled it open. Within moments, he had it lit and ready. He pulled steadily on the end, letting the smoke curl from his lips.

"Come here," he instructed, resting his hip to the ledge. Elizabeth set down the glass and obeyed. Harrison hesitated.

"Well, show me," she said quietly. "How do you do it?"

"I almost regret my words to you that day at the cottage," he said, not handing her the cigar. He lifted his fingers to stroke her cheek tenderly. "Sometimes I wish I could take them back. I fear they have ruined you."

"Ruined me?" Elizabeth shook her head. "No, they have saved me. Don't you see? They gave me the courage to go after what I want. I've been..."

"What?" he prodded. "What have you been?"

"Freed," she said. "Your words freed me."

"And what about my friendship?"

The smoke curled from the lit cigar pulled out the opened window into the evening sky. They ignored it.

"What about it?" Elizabeth's eyes were held captive by his. The soft glow of blue moonlight edged his face and she found herself wanting to touch him. His shirt blew softly in the breeze, molding and pulling from his stomach and chest. He looked so relaxed, calm, handsome. He made her heart race and stop all at once. It was a strange feeling.

"How do you feel about it?"

"I value it," she said honestly.

"Only value?"

"What would you have me say, my lord?" Elizabeth questioned. Her head tilted to the side.

"Here," Harrison said instead. His lids lowered and he held out the cigar end to her. He instructed, "Put it between your lips and breath in, gentle and slow."

Elizabeth took it. Her lips parted and she slipped the rounded tip into her mouth. Harrison's gaze narrowed. His breath caught. The edge of Elizabeth's lip pulled up. But, then, she inhaled slowly. Her face instantly turned a shade of green and she coughed, a raw hacking sound.

Harrison grabbed the cigar from her and tapped it out on the side of the house. Pulling her forward, he thrust her face toward the fresh air.

"I warned you that it wasn't a good idea," he said.

"You could... have... warned me... that it was... like breathing... fire," she gasped, coughing between words. "I need a drink."

Harrison rushed to get her the brandy. She took a sip and the coughing subsided.

"I think I prefer brandy to cigars," she said when she could again talk. "I don't know what you see in them."

"It's an acquired taste."

"Well, then I shall acquire a taste for it," she murmured. When Harrison's brow rose in question, she lifted an arm to his neck. Her eyes dipped to his lips as she said, "Let me taste it on you."

Harrison smiled. He leaned down, pulling her closer into his arms.

Elizabeth moaned lightly, anticipating the touch of him. The taste of fine brandy on her tongue mingled with the unique flavor of him against her lips.

"I love..." Elizabeth began without thinking. Her heart nearly stopped, but she artfully added, "The feel of you. You're so hot, firm."

Harrison groaned against her mouth, deepening the kiss. Pulling back, he said, "And I love your skin, so soft, silky, smooth. Take off that gown for me, let me watch you undress."

Elizabeth stepped back. Harrison tossed off his shirt. Then, crossing to the bed, he pulled the breeches off his hips and crawled naked onto the mattress. He laid back, his gaze watching expectantly. His arousal was already thick with need, standing up from his body. He ignored it.

Elizabeth slowly pulled the nightgown over her

head. Her gaze lowered as she tossed it aside, only to lift back to watch for his approval.

Harrison studied her slender frame. He licked his lips. His breathing deepened. His gaze dropped to the soft bed of curls between her legs. "Touch yourself for me."

His eyes were too warm for her not to obey. She didn't feel embarrassment with him. He made her feel as if she could do anything, that nothing else mattered when it was the two of them. She trusted him more than she'd ever trusted anyone.

Elizabeth lightly cupped her breasts, massaging them as he watched. She pinched the nipples as he often did. A jolt of pleasure racked over her and a soft moan fell from her lips. Harrison didn't move. His shaft seemed to lengthen before her eyes. His gaze followed the movements of her hands.

Elizabeth ran her hands over her sensitive neck. She pulled the pins from her hair, freeing it. It fell in waves, tickling her already sensitive flesh.

Harrison took his hand from behind his head and moved it along his stomach. Elizabeth stopped in her self exploration to watch him. He let his fingers journey down the light trail of hair beneath his navel before reaching his towering erection.

She gazed eagerly at him, enthralled as he stroked his

hard length. He gripped at the top over the smooth head and rubbed down along the shaft. She'd never seen anything so erotically stirring in her life. She moved her hands down her stomach, eager to try. She bit her lip, smiling as he nodded at her to continue her descending trail.

Elizabeth stroked herself for him. Harrison groaned. His gaze fixed wildly on her finger as it dipped into the soft curls.

"Come onto the bed," he said, his voice rough. "Come closer. I want to see more."

Elizabeth crawled on the bed. She straddled his knees, kneeling above him. His hand pumped faster, gripping tight to his hard shaft. His gaze moved to her hips, urging her to continue her naughty little show.

Elizabeth thrust her fingers against the sensitive nub guarding her heated opening. She moaned, keeping time with his quickening movements. Soon she was panting, moaning, gasping for breath. Her eyes became hazy. She frantically grabbed a breast, becoming mindless with the sight of him. She couldn't take her gaze from his beautiful body.

"Stroke inside," he ordered. He moved his free hand to cup the soft globes beneath his thick arousal.

Elizabeth obeyed and was rewarded as her fingers

slipped inside. She trembled with the threat of complete fulfillment.

"Don't stop," Harrison said. His stomach tensed but he held himself back, slowing his fingers. "I want to watch you bring yourself to full pleasure."

Elizabeth couldn't have stopped if she wanted to. Sweat beaded on her flesh. Tremors racked her body as her release racked over her. It was pleasant but not nearly as strong as when Harrison was in her.

"I want more." She leaned over him to crawl along his body.

"Turn around," he ordered.

Elizabeth blinked in confusion.

"Trust me," he urged gently. "I won't hurt you —*ever*."

"I know." Elizabeth wondered at the softness of his tone. She shivered, turning.

Harrison groaned to see her backside pushed toward him. He hadn't even begun to fulfill the fantasies he had of her. Coming up behind her, he rubbed a finger into her slick opening, stroking her until her feminine moisture flooded his fingers. Only when she gasped his name, over and over, did he guide his shaft to her body. He thrust hard into her tight opening.

Elizabeth cried out as he filled her. She rocked her body

back into his, meeting his thrusts. At first he took her slow, enjoying the slick glide of her tight passage over him as he taught her how deep and strong he could go into her body. But, soon, the torment was too much and he needed to find his release. Controlling her hips, he withdrew and plunged against her, faster, harder, deeper, fitting within her.

Their bodies became one as they both climaxed in unison. She gripped the coverlet. Harrison pulled his fingers to her mouth, stifling her loud cry. Her trembling body clenched tightly around him as he exploded to fill her with his release.

Weakly, his head fell along her back, his body nestled warmly inside hers. He pulled her back onto him, wrapping her in his arms from behind. He held her tight, nuzzling her neck.

"Marry me," he said softly. "Say you'll be my wife."

Elizabeth stiffened, though pleasure still tried to curl in her stomach. He was embedded deep inside her. She couldn't speak.

Harrison kissed her neck and she trembled violently, feeling it all the way to her toes. "Tell me you'll marry me. I want to hold you like this for the rest of our days. I want to show you things. I want to give you grand adventures. I want to take you all over the world and make love to you in every country. Life will be too tiresome without you by my side to share it."

It wasn't how Harrison wished the words to come out but he couldn't think.

"I'm not your plaything," she said, struggling to break his hold. "I wouldn't marry to ease your boredom, my lord."

Harrison held tighter, not letting her go. "If we are married, there will be no need to have an affair. We'll be with each other and no one will question what we do. You'll be rich, titled."

Elizabeth's heart beat quickened. He said everything she would hear but the one thing she needed to hear, to believe from him. She needed his love and she doubted a rogue like him was capable of giving it. She broke away from his hold.

"How dare you?" Tears streamed over her cheeks as she pulled away. "What we had was a perfect arrangement and you ruined it."

"Elizabeth," he began. "Wait, I'm not finishe—"

"I think you are, my lord," Elizabeth said. "I may have come to you in friendship but I'm not a bauble for you to collect. I'm not a new toy for you to play with until you're bored with me."

"So I'm good enough for you to bed but not to be your husband." The words were cold, flat.

"Honestly, my lord. What kind of marriage could you possibly give me?" she asked, her voice calm, unnervingly somber. "How soon until your eye wanders back to the maid?"

"Nothing happened with the maid." He growled and made a move to grab her. She leapt from the bed.

Elizabeth reached for her nightgown, ready to pull it over her head. She trembled. She needed to get away from him. His proposal stung. He tried to buy her with his title, tempting her with her newfound freedom. He didn't want her. He wanted a partner in mischief. And, though his offer was tempting, her heart demanded more —a more he couldn't give her.

"My lord," Elizabeth stated calmly, whirling about, clutching the nightgown to her chest. Her arms were in the sleeves but she didn't move to pull it over her head. Harrison was off the bed and she backed away from him. "I won't marry you. I'm sure if you stop to think logically about this, you will come to understand what a grave mistake such a union would be. I know you hold no stock in love, for how could you? I don't condemn you for—"

"You think to know me so well?" he asked, incredulous. "You presume too much about my character."

"All the more reason for us not to join. I have only known you a week," she said. Seeing he wasn't going to pounce, she pulled the nightgown over her head. When she looked at him, he was still gloriously naked. She wanted to let her gaze roam over his delectable frame. She forced her eyes to stay on his handsome face.

"And I have known you longer."

"You mean you feel as—" she began.

"No, I mean that I have known you for a year," he stated. Harrison's own eyes drifted over her shoulder to the painting beneath the blanket.

"A year? Are you mad? We have never been introduced—"

"I saw you in the garden," he said quietly, turning his eyes back to her. "You were dancing in the rain."

Elizabeth didn't know what to make of his unreadable look.

"You chased a kitten and it ran away from you. And I saw you in the rain. I knew then that I wanted to have you," he said. "You were rumored to be so damned respectable, prudish. I wanted to—I wanted to be with you. I wanted to make you my lover. I wanted to show you—"

"You wanted to corrupt me." Elizabeth shook her head, thinking to understand. "I'm a game to you."

"What?"

"You somehow tricked my brother into an invitation and you came to seduce me. What a fool you must think of me. I thought you were offering friendship, but this is a game to see how far I would go. You have no intention of marrying me. Even your asking it was false."

"Let me explain," he pleaded.

"There is nothing to explain. You wished to corrupt me and so you have, my lord," Elizabeth sneered. "With your words you have turned this lady into a whore. I hope you enjoyed your conquest, but this affair is over. I have grown bored with you and I wish to discover if other men—"

"Elizabeth," Harrison said in warning.

"What?" She forced a laugh. "Did you think I was falling for you? Please. I admit your motives do disappoint me. However, now that I'm ruined, I shall live life to the absolute fullest. There is no reason I shouldn't go to other men—so long as I'm *discreet*."

Harrison's face turned red with anger.

Elizabeth rushed to the door. The earl was behind her but her look stopped him. "I apologize for not being more of a conquest for you. Good luck on your future endeavors."

"Elizabeth."

"I want you out of this house by tomorrow morning. Tell Thomas you have grown bored with the country and wish to get back to your women in the city. Tell him this or I'll tell him you attacked me. I have seen your affection for my brother and hope that it's sincerer than your friendship to me. Either way, I doubt you would want to fight him in a duel. What would society think of you killing their premier artist? Not even your wealth could bury that scandal."

Elizabeth felt her nose burning with unshed tears as she flung open the door. She was bluffing. She'd never put Thomas in harm's way like that but the earl didn't need to know it. He moved behind her but she didn't stop. She should have known that what they had was too good to be true. She'd wanted to believe he cared for her, just a little. But his words rang in her head. He saw her as a conquest, an adventure. He'd heard she was a prude, saw that she was fair to look at, and had wanted to corrupt her.

By the time she arrived in her bedroom, she was weeping. She locked the door behind her, flinging herself on her bed. The misery of her broken heart hit her with such force that she couldn't breathe. She doubted she would ever be whole again.

Harrison watched her go. He started to follow her but stopped. Grabbing the brandy snifter from the dresser, he threw it toward the unlit fireplace. The glass shattered.

He didn't hesitate as he grabbed a large, broken shard. Strolling to the painting, he tore the blanket off it, ready to strike. His arm lifted, a yell frozen on his angry lips. He couldn't do it. Sinking to his knees, he stared at the canvas.

The figure of Elizabeth knelt on the ground, frozen and unmoving with her hands buried in her face. The pistol lay next to her, abandoned. The riding crop had fallen from the stone and even the bluebells seemed to be withering on the vine.

The glass slipped from his fingers and the earl knelt before the portrait. Grabbing the frame, he shook it violently. His voice a whisper, he demanded, "What is it you want from me?"

19

Elizabeth rubbed her eyes as she made her way to the library. Thomas wanted to see her. She guessed that he was going to be off to London with the earl and Mr. Turner, so that they may share in the ride together. It was just as well. She wanted to be alone for a long, long time and it would be impossible to nurse her wounds with Thomas' artistic gaze studying her every emotion.

Knocking quietly, she entered before being summonsed. Seeing her brother, his head down on his desk, she couldn't help her small smile. If she had her guess, he'd spent the night in the studio with Mr. Turner preparing for the show. Seeing a spatter of red paint in his hair, she chuckled softly.

"Thomas?" she asked quietly, ready to turn and leave him to his rest.

To her surprise, his head pulled up to look at her. He did indeed look as if he hadn't slept but there was something strange in the way he studied her. Her stomach tightened. He looked as if death rode on his heels, so pale and gray was his face.

"Thomas? What is it? Has something happened? Has... someone been hurt?" Elizabeth rushed to go to him but his uneasy look held her back.

"The earl has asked for your hand and I have granted it. You're to be married as soon as possible."

For a moment, Elizabeth blinked, not believing to understand his words. Her legs weakened and she stumbled to fall into a chair. "Thomas? I apologize. I think I misheard you. I thought you said I was to marry the earl."

"Yes as soon as it can be arranged," Thomas said. "I have already spoken to Lord Wrotham and have sent notice to the papers in London."

"Surely, you jest," Elizabeth said. This couldn't be real.

"So he's not who you would've chosen for yourself?"

"No, of course not." Elizabeth wondered at the surprise in his tired face. "Why ever would you think such a thing, Thomas?"

"Because he knows."

Elizabeth couldn't move as she heard the earl's low voice behind her. She shivered. A look of horror came over her as she saw the truth of it on Thomas' face. Her brother couldn't meet her eye. Instead, he looked at his desk.

"I don't understand," Elizabeth said unconvincingly. She tried to remain calm, though her heart raced and her head spun. She couldn't look at the earl but she felt him behind her. "Knows what?"

Harrison's hand slid onto her shoulder and she tensed under its pressing weight. "Knows about us, darling."

Elizabeth jumped. The endearment didn't sound like that of a lover, or even a friend. She finally managed to look at Harrison's face. His eyes were dark, emotionless pits as they stared at her.

"What did you say?" she ground out, glaring at him. "I deny it, Thomas. Whatever this rogue has said, I deny it. You, my lord earl, have overstayed your welcome here. I demand that you leave at once and never come back."

"If he leaves," Thomas said quietly. He observed the two lovers. "Then you go with him."

Elizabeth shook her head in denial. "Thomas, why? What have I done to deserve this treatment from you?"

"I saw you, Elizabeth. I saw you with my own eyes," Thomas yelled. His body shook with passion as he stood from his chair. He glared at both of them, hurt, confused. Lowering his tone, he repeated, "I saw you."

"Surely, you don't know what you saw," she said. "Please, don't make me marry him. Give me to anyone but him."

Harrison watched, feeling as if she slapped him with each word. Slowly, her dark eyes turned to him, helpless, scared, angry. She shook violently and swayed on her feet.

"You chose him, Elizabeth, not I," Thomas said. "Even now you might carry his child. I won't have you publicly shamed for I know how you value your reputation. To be humiliated in such a way would destroy you. I'm sorry. But you will be married with much haste and little ceremony. I have already dispatched Mr. Turner to London with the rumor that I merely forgot to post the bans of your engagement a year ago. It will be quite the scandal but I believe I'll be forgiven. Disorganized, hapless artists are fashionable at the moment. With Lord Wrotham's less than usual behavior this last year, it will be believed the engagement was already in place. And, with your reputation for being reserved, it will be assumed you demanded a small, quiet wedding."

Elizabeth flinched. She looked helplessly from one man to the other. "How soon?"

"I believe it can be arranged for Friday," Thomas said. None of them looked happy. There was an odd tension in the room. "Have your plans ready by then, Elizabeth."

Elizabeth's eyes turned hard. Looking at the earl, she said, "You may force me to be a bride but I won't be a happy one. If you wish to plan this nightmare, have at it. I want little part in it."

Elizabeth strode from the library, refusing to cry until she was out of their sight.

Harrison watched her go. Swallowing, he turned to Thomas. "Thomas—?"

"Leave me, Harry," Thomas said wearily. He turned his back to stare out the window.

Harrison knew his friend felt betrayed and he was sorry for it. He also knew that Thomas hated himself for having to force his sister's hand. Quietly, the earl said, "I'll take care of her."

"I know," Thomas answered. He glanced over his shoulder. "But perhaps you should try telling her that."

"I would. I have tried. But she doesn't want to hear me."

20

Several days passed and Elizabeth avoided her new fiancé as if he carried the plague. She refused to come to breakfast or dinner, often rising so early that she was out riding with a picnic before the others awoke. She'd stay out all morning and afternoon, never telling where she went but for the vaguest of directions. When she returned, Thomas would look at her sadly. She could barely meet his eyes before running up to her room. Each night, Thomas had a tray of food sent to her. She was grateful for it.

On the first night, Harrison had come to her door, knocking softly asking if he may enter. Her door was locked and she didn't answer, no matter that he stood outside it for a little over half of an hour. He hadn't tried again since.

Elizabeth felt awful. Her heart ached for herself and her conscience ached for the earl, though she tried to tell herself she hated him. He would make a fair husband and the passion was there between them but how long would such a thing last? How long until she saw his eyes turn to another? How long before her heart shattered, leaving her empty? She should have run far away from him that first day by the cottage when he suggested she live a double life. She should have known better.

Looking back, she did know better.

Looking back, she knew that it was the earl who captured her interest, not only with his words—though they pleased her. He accepted her for who she was, not forcing her into a role.

For that, she'd fallen in love with him.

For that, she was now to be punished for the rest of her life.

The cottage ruins stood before her as did the bridge she loved so much. It was the first time she'd been back since she started her foolish pact with Lord Wrotham. To look at it now, only a week and a half later, she felt strange.

Sliding down from her sidesaddle, Elizabeth landed neatly on the ground. She left her mare to graze, not caring if it ran off without her. Today was to be her wedding day and as she had said, she hadn't lifted a finger in the planning of it. She couldn't bear to. As far as she knew, nothing special had been planned and no hour set. The local parish only had one vicar, so it was doubtful he cared at what hour he wed them.

Looking down, she saw the white gown that was left in her chambers the night before. It was a simply elegant affair of soft hem pleats and stamped velvet trim. A small bonnet with a long veil flowed over her back, covering the ringlets of her hair, which spilled along her shoulders. Her maid was only too happy to inform her that the earl had ordered it from London. She took little time to wonder at his thoughtfulness.

Crossing over the field, toward the little stream, she sighed. She couldn't go home and face the earl or her wedding, not yet. And as she looked over the distance, she didn't know if she would ever get the courage to go home again.

Harrison could barely breathe as he urged his stallion over the long field. The horse's legs stretched and pounded as they ate away at the distance. He had to find her. Never had he dreamt she would abandon him at the altar. He didn't know what he would say to her once he found her. His fist clenched in outrage. It was possible he wouldn't say anything at all.

He neared the cottage ruins, the sleeves of his white linen shirt ruffling in the strong wind beneath his dark blue waistcoat. He'd discarded his jacket when it was reported that Elizabeth wasn't in her room. Instantly, he consulted the portrait, not caring that Thomas was right on his heels.

When he asked the portrait where she was, Thomas had gasped as if he were insane. Only after seeing for himself the changes wrought upon his work did he understand its mystical power. No longer did Elizabeth stand by the broken wall in the garden. She was before the old cottage.

Harrison saw her mare and urged his horse faster. Coming up alongside it, he finally slowed. Her horse startled nervously and ambled away from their intrusion, trotting off into the distant field only to stop and watch him for a brief instant before turning to graze again.

Harrison swung roughly off his mount. He found Elizabeth on the bridge and strode straight for her. Her eyes glared in his direction, watching him approach.

Elizabeth watched the earl come for her. How dare he intrude upon her solitude? But, seeing his angry face, her heart fluttered. She took a quick step back and then another.

"What are you doing here?" he asked, nearing her.

Elizabeth didn't answer.

"You left me waiting at the altar for you," Harrison charged. She flinched ready to fight him off.

To her amazement, his hands lifted and pulled her face roughly to his in a searing kiss. Elizabeth moaned in surprise. Harrison's tongue invaded her mouth, leaving her breathless and weak. She tried to resist but she couldn't. Her hands rode up his shoulders to settle around his neck. She pressed her length into him, feeling the familiar pull of his strong body.

Harrison ripped away from her with a growl. She blinked, confused as he stepped back. His chest heaved as did hers.

"How did you find me?" she asked.

"Your portrait, it showed me," Harrison said, knowing she didn't understand. He didn't have the strength to explain it to her. "Why did you leave me? Why won't you marry me?"

"My lord," Elizabeth began. She tasted him on her lips.

"No, you feel for me," he said, beginning to pace. He tossed his hands up in the air. "I don't understand. What would you have of me? Tell me what to do to make you feel anything for me. Tell me what to say and I'll say it. Do you want me to change? I'll change... I..."

Elizabeth felt tears coming to her eyes. She didn't want pretty words. She wanted all of him.

"Tell me how to make you love me." Harrison couldn't stand it any longer. He came before her, his troubled eyes pleading with her. "Tell me how to make you feel as I feel for you."

A tear spilled over her cheek and she dashed it away. Her lips trembled. "I don't wish to marry you, my lord. Please, let us not go through with it."

"Am I so horrible that you can't find it in your heart to be with me? Am I such an ill-suited match? Why won't you have me?"

"Because you can't love me!" Elizabeth yelled. Instantly, she gripped her fingers over her mouth. She shook violently, backing away from him, stumbling over the boards of the bridge in her haste. Her words were a whisper as she finished, "It's not possible. You only love yourself."

"How can you not know?" he asked softly. He let the full force of his torment into his eyes, his face, his voice. "I can only love you. I saw you in the garden, dancing in the rain and I fell madly in love with you. How can you not know it?"

"How could I?" Her limbs shook but this time it was with unsure pleasure. She looked at his expression and she wanted to believe him.

"There has been no one else in my bed for over a year and there has never been anyone else in my heart." He went to her again and gathered her up into his arms. "I love you, Elizabeth. I meant it when I said I wanted you to be my wife. I know that you don't care for me but you want me. And, if you give me a chance, I'll make you happy. I'll deny you nothing in this world. I'll give you everything I have."

Elizabeth glanced over the earl's shoulder. She noticed Thomas on his horse as well as Mr. Turner. Next to them was the local vicar.

Harrison swooped down on his knee. He pulled a ring from his waistcoat and held it up to her. "Please, Elizabeth, marry me. You never gave mc the opportunity to ask you properly before, so I'm asking you now. Complete me. Be my wife."

Elizabeth looked at him and then to the approaching horses. Her mouth trembling, she bid him, "Stand up."

Harrison did, frowning. His face hardened and closed. His eyes turned mournful as if his heart broke inside him.

"Kiss me," she said softly. "Just keep kissing me."

Elizabeth burst forward, grabbing his face in her hands. She plied him with soft kisses, sprinkling them over his face. She pulled back, smiling up at him through her tears.

"Why didn't you tell me you loved me before?" she asked. "That's all I've been waiting to hear. I don't care about the title, the money, the adventures. You're all the adventure I want. I love you, Harrison. How could you not know that? I've loved you since you first stepped out of your carriage and smiled at me."

Elizabeth touched his dimple.

"But—"

"Foolish man," she said quietly. "Why do you think I tried so hard to put you off?"

"Is everything settled?"

Elizabeth and Harrison looked at Thomas. He stood at the end of the bridge, looking them over, taking in Elizabeth's tear-stained face—so full of emotions he'd never seen in her, never dreamt of seeing—to Harrison's wide grin.

"Yes," Elizabeth said.

Harrison looked at her and she lifted her finger for him to give her the ring. He grinned, staring into her eyes as he slipped it onto her finger, and he didn't stop staring at her until the vicar married them right there on the bridge. Mr. Turner and Thomas stood by as witnesses.

After the short ceremony, Harrison kissed his wife and swooped her up into his arms. Grinning, he turned to their small group of guests. "Thank you but kindly leave now. I go to take my wife on our honeymoon."

Elizabeth wrapped her arms around his neck. Her skirts blew gently against them. "Honeymoon?"

Harrison nodded toward the cottage. "I believe we have some unfinished business here."

Thomas quickly turned to shoo the vicar and Mr. Turner away. Then, watching as Harrison carried his sister off toward the abandoned cottage, he called, "Until later tonight then?"

"Yes, Thomas," Elizabeth called, waving him away. Then, leaning to kiss her husband, she said, "I can't believe this."

"What?" Harrison teased. "I told you I would take care of you. This is the best accommodation the field has to offer. Only the best honeymoon for my wife."

"Oh," she said in feigned anger, slapping his strong shoulder. "Can't you take anything seriously?"

"Why?" he murmured, carrying her over the threshold. He kissed her again, pouring his heart into hers. "When the world will take things seriously enough for the both of us?"

EPILOGUE

Elizabeth looked up from where she lay against her husband's naked chest. Her eyes found the blanket thrown over the chair. They stayed in the Caldwell guestroom, preparing to leave for their home in the morning. Their trunks were already loaded and waiting for them below stairs.

Elizabeth yawned, purring contentedly. Harrison had made love to her until her body could barely move from exhaustion and then he'd made love to her again. It took Harrison and Thomas a long while to convince Elizabeth that her portrait was mystical but after such ardent pleas, she finally conceded to believe them.

"I want to see it," Elizabeth said.

Harrison followed her eyes to the portrait. She'd yet

to look at it. He grinned, kissing her deeply. She moaned, feeling her body stir to him.

"You may have whatever you wish, darling," he said softly. He spanked her lightly on her naked backside and crawled from her arms. Crossing naked over to the covered portrait, Harrison hesitated.

Elizabeth eyed his handsome form, moving to follow him. Wrapping her arms around his waist, she leaned into him and peeked from beneath his arm. "I still think I'm a fool for believing you."

"I swear it's all true," he answered. "Look for yourself."

Harrison whipped the blanket off the portrait, revealing it to the soft blue moonlight. But it wasn't Elizabeth who gasped to see it. Harrison leaned forward, amazed to see the portrait as it once was, with Elizabeth standing by the broken stone wall, surrounded by roses.

"I swear," he began.

"Look," Elizabeth said pointing. She knelt and touched the surface. Her fingers glanced over her face. "I look happy. Did Thomas repaint it?"

"I told you, it's magic." Harrison joined her on the floor.

Indeed, the portrait smiled secretively out at them, the expression not reserved as it once was but content.

"Look at your hand," Harrison said, pointing to

where they should have been clasped together. Instead, they rested flat against her belly. The hint of a wedding ring glinted on her finger. His eyes rounded and he looked at her stomach, only to bring his hand to rest there.

"Do you think I'm pregnant?" Elizabeth asked.

Harrison growled, playfully tackling her to the floor. "I think... no, I know that I have everything I could ever wish for, right here with you, my wife."

"Oh," Elizabeth gasped. It was the only sound she managed as Harrison began kissing her.

The End

New York Times & *USA TODAY* Bestselling Author

Michelle loves to travel and try new things, whether it's a paranormal investigation of an old Vaudeville Theatre or climbing Mayan temples in Belize. She believes life is an adventure fueled by copious amounts of coffee.

Newly relocated to the American South, Michelle is involved in various film and documentary projects with her talented director husband. She is mom to a fantastic artist. And she's managed by a dog and cat who make sure she's meeting her deadlines.

For the most part she can be found wearing pajama pants and working in her office. There may or may not be dancing. It's all part of the creative process.

Come say hello! Michelle loves talking with readers on social media!

www.MichellePillow.com

- facebook.com/AuthorMichellePillow
- twitter.com/michellepillow
- instagram.com/michellempillow
- bookbub.com/authors/michelle-m-pillow
- goodreads.com/Michelle_Pillow
- amazon.com/author/michellepillow
- youtube.com/michellepillow
- pinterest.com/michellepillow

Gothic Regency Romance
A love story that defies perception...

When the willfully independent Isabel Drake refuses to marry the man her parents want her to, her mother decides as punishment she will be forced to take lessons on how to be a proper lady. But the man sent to instruct her makes her feel anything but proper. Her attraction to Mr. Weston is instant, but the confusing man seems set in keeping her in her place—even if she detects he feels something for her.

But things are not what they seem at Rothfield Park or with her new tutor. With Mr. Weston's arrival there comes an abundance of unrested spirits. Suddenly, Isabel doesn't know who is alive and who is dead. Why have they come now? And what are they trying frantically to tell her? Isabel must discover the truth about the eerie night mist that surrounds the manor before it comes to claim everyone she holds dear—including her Mr. Weston.

Extended Excerpt

Rothfield Park, England, 1812

"My heart pounded in a violent fit, and the child would not quit screaming." Jane Drake's words flowed in a rush at her oldest sister. Her round eyes shone through the glass frames of her spectacles, echoing the strength of her conviction. "I swear to you, Isabel. It was real. There are unrested spirits at Rothfield Park."

"It was a dream," Isabel assured her, remaining calm. Jane was a sweet girl, and Isabel loved her dearly. However, her bookish sister had somewhat of a wild imagination when it came to Rothfield Park.

"I'm not explaining it well." Jane's usually meek expression had stiffened with fright. Absently, she pushed the sliding spectacles up her nose. Her pink linen gown flowed as she paced. The color reflected in the flush of her cheeks. The high empire waist was belted with a dark pink sash and matching ribbons bound up her dark brown hair. Despite the richness of her gown,

Jane had an indifferent air to her manners, an untidiness that was rather endearing.

Isabel sighed. Her concerned blue eyes met her sister's wide brown ones. She had half a mind to reprimand the servants for telling the girl such fanciful tales upon the family's arrival to the home. Patting her sister's cheek with a soft, kidskin glove, she whispered, "Oh, Jane, we have let Rothfield Park for nigh six whole months. If spirits were lurking about the manor they would have made themselves known before now."

"But I think they *are* making themselves known. I have heard them moving about this past week," Jane insisted. "I know there are more than one. There is the terrified child. And a man—"

"Jane, I will hear no more of this. Quit trying to frighten me." Isabel shivered, disliking talk of the supernatural. She had no idea why Jane had been so apprehensive lately, but it needed to stop. Then an idea struck her. "Did you just read that new *shilling shocker* novel that Harriet sent to you from London?"

"Yes. But, I—" Jane began.

"Shh," Isabel hushed. "Therein lies your problem. You have been staying up late reading in bed, haven't you? Oh, Jane, and to waste such a gifted mind on such rubbish."

Jane merely nodded at the loving correction.

Satisfied that her sister's fears were for naught, Isabel relaxed. She smiled at the girl and gave her an impish wink to cheer her. Jane was only sixteen and still very impressionable. Harriet loved to exploit the youngest Drake's fantasies by giving useless gifts.

"You had best be careful when speaking of such things, especially to Mother. She will have Reverend Campbell here in an instant to exorcise this house from demons." Isabel paused mischievously. "Can you imagine such a thing? The Scotsman would—"

"Issie, please," Jane broke in before her sister could say anything that would insult the poor vicar. "He is a man of God."

"He is a self-righteous prig who I believe is taken to drink."

Jane frowned and turned her attention to the floor.

The fine muslin of her blue and cream gown swished as Isabel moved past her sister to the sideboard. Seeing the customary tray of pastries her parents had the servants set out for breakfast, she ignored the stacked plates, chose a scone and took a bite, leaning over the tray and using her gloved hand to catch any crumbs that fell. She noticed her distorted reflection in polished silver, and she liked the way her prettily coiffured hair bounced around her head in gentle, dark curls.

"Allow me, Miss Drake." A maid rushed forward,

shaking her head. The servant grabbed a plate and held it under the crumbling breakfast.

Isabel sighed. With a heavenward roll of her eyes, she relinquished the pastry to the fine china. The maid rushed the plate to the table, pulling back a chair for her mistress. Isabel dusted her gloves and waved the woman away with an annoyed toss of her hand.

"Miss Jane?" The maid gestured to the food.

Jane shook her head in denial. "No, thank you."

The maid backed from the room with a polite curtsey.

"Issie," Jane said when they were once again alone. "Please, you must believe me. There was a child in my chamber last night. I could hardly sleep from the fright of it."

"Oh, my most prudent sister, I would believe you if the idea were not so fantastic of a notion. But I think I would be more apt to believe you if you told me my horse grew another set of legs overnight. This house is not haunted. And, hate the isolation of Rothfield as I do, I cannot give credence to such a conjecture."

"You think me a silly girl, don't you?" Jane asked.

"No, sweet Jane." Isabel smiled tenderly, a look saved only for her sister. Jane was her truest friend. "I don't."

Viscount Sutherfeld, their father, had moved his three daughters far from London and the influence of high London society, believing it had been breeding insensible ideas into the girls' heads. The middle sister, Harriet Drake, was the first to protest to their Aunt Mildred so that the old woman took pity and invited her to stay in her home in London. Once a month they would receive a dutiful letter from Harriet gloating about the fine society she was keeping and her hopes of snagging a suitably rich husband of consequence. The thought brought a frown to Isabel's features. Jane looked at her in worry.

"I do not think you are silly," Isabel asserted. "I think you are bored, as you must be in such a place as this. Too bad a regiment of soldiers will not come to stay in Haventon so that we might for once give a ball."

"I do not mind it so much," Jane allowed. She had been out for only one season. That one season was enough to convince the littlest Drake she would much prefer to stay in the country. Scratching thoughtfully at her mousy brown hair, she pushed her spectacles up on her nose. "I should not like it with Aunt Mildred. I do hate having to make conversation with such men as are at balls. I never know what to say to them, and they never seem to be listening to me unless I speak of you or Harriet."

"You do say the strangest things," Isabel mused.

Clearly deciding it best to change the subject, Jane

forgot her ghosts for a moment. "You look very prettily done up, Issie. Is Mr. Tanner coming to call on you?"

"Yes." Isabel smiled, instantly disregarding her oncoming melancholy with the name of her gallant suitor. Sighing wistfully, she thought of his dark blond hair and laughing brown eyes. Her Edward was always in fine spirits, and he made it impossible to think of anything contrary to happiness. "He is. I am sure he will seek permission from Father soon. And, though he does not have a lot of money, I think with my dowry and his smart investing, we will be reasonably well off. Already I have expressed my desire to go to London and Bath. I have it on good authority that he might have expectations of his own though he would not tell me the exact details."

Jane tried to smile, but couldn't. She often said she did not want to think of Isabel leaving her. "And what of the Colonel? He seems very smitten."

"Colonel Wallace?" Isabel shot in surprise. Her hand fluttered to her chest. "Please, Jane. Whatever made you think of the Colonel?"

"When you were sleeping this morning, he came to visit Father. I do not flatter myself that he came for me," Jane said.

Isabel did not pay attention to the jealous tinge in her sister's tone. She turned to glance out the side window overlooking the front drive. The long, straight, gravel road disappeared into the distance, hiding all of their neighbor's homes from sight. Along each side of the drive were numerous shrubs, sculpted to perfection.

"Is he still here?" Isabel asked, hating that she might be forced to entertain the quiet man. He was as sparing with his smiles as he was his praise. She should abhor having such a man as he for company, let alone as a husband. The only thing recommending Colonel Wallace besides the fact that his uncle was the owner of Rothfield Park, and in essence, their landlord, was that he was rich in his own right. Once the Colonel's uncle died, he would come into even greater wealth. Isabel shivered. What was wealth if it brought with it no happiness?

"No, I believe he must have gone away by now. Even so, Father wished me to send you to the library when you were of a mind to come from your room. I suppose I should have told you right off, but I wanted you to myself before he put you in a mood."

"It is not Father who I find to be disagreeable. It is Mother." Isabel naughtily grimaced as she walked past her sister toward the large paneled doors. Resting her gloved hand on the mahogany, she grumbled, "Too bad she could not have gone to London with Harriet. Maybe, you should speak to her and convince her to go. I would like the country better if she were not in it."

Jane did not bother to scold. Instead, she smiled. Isabel and her mother were rarely on speaking terms. It was not unusual for weeks to pass with hardly a word uttered between the two of them. Isabel turned around to face her.

"If it would please you, we can exchange rooms. I swear I have never heard so much as a single moan in my chamber," Isabel said.

Jane's eyes lit up. "But that is because my room is in the section of the house that was rebuilt after the fire. I am sure something tragic happened that night. I would very much like to help the poor child."

"Nonsense." Isabel refused to pay heed to such things as ghosts. "But, we will trade if it helps you to sleep easier."

"Yes, thank you."

Isabel nodded, forgetting the bothersome business as soon as she left the dining room.

Rothfield Park was an old estate, having been renamed for the Marquis of Rothfield who, in some sixty years past, had restored and expanded the place to one of grandeur and good taste. Soon after having finished the very last detail of the very last room, however, a fire had mysteriously started and burned down a sizeable section of the house. The flames were said to have killed a few servants and a child. It was also rumored that the meticulous Marquis went mad at having all his work destroyed and soon after died himself, leaving the estate and title to a cousin—Colonel Wallace's uncle.

No wonder Jane believes this house is haunted, thought Isabel in hard-pressed amusement. She barely gave credence to the story. She assumed it was exaggerated for the sake of bored country folk. *How else are the good people of Haventon going to get the high society of London to visit them way up north in the middle of nowhere?*

Still, even Isabel had to admit that, for the generously lenient price they paid for the letting of the house, it was a wondrous home. She could not understand why the Marquis would have built it in such an area, but nevertheless appreciated his eye for details, from the tall white walls of the main hall, trimmed and outlined with mahogany, to the expansive archways and shutters of the same wood, to the pristine marble floors of the adequately sized ballroom. Only a few pieces of furniture had arrived with the Drake family, the aged lines oddly out of place with the understated elegance of the furnishing that belonged with the house. The gentle curves of the Rothfield collection were of an older style, not the Palladian style of the modern day, but still gracious and befitting a great estate.

Rich tapestry lined the chairs and settees. Candleholders and fireplaces, sweeping draperies and paned windows, all graced their proper places. Strewn along the carved stone mantles, and wooden tabletops were an immense variety of vases, sculptures, and clocks. Large portraits of people and dogs lined the vast walls, hung on damask and Genoa velvet. Their clothing was antiquated and their faces so unrecognizable that Isabel found they were hardly worth looking at except out of boredom.

Along the east wing were the bedrooms, each large and exceptional. Isabel imagined they were not so fine as they should have been, belonging to a Marquis, but they were well enough for the Drake family's needs. The bedrooms had fireplaces and huge four-poster beds, potted plants, and sturdy furniture. Drawing rooms and dressing rooms adjoined each one.

The house was built in the shape of a 'U' with a paved courtyard and working fountain in the center. Beyond the house were the dense woods fanning in one direction—great for hunting deer her father claimed though he never hunted—and cutting through the woods was a stream.

Between the house and woods were beautiful land-scaped gardens, not so well manicured as one would desire, but adequate. There was a beauty to the untamed vining of roses in the spring and summer, and to the broken cobblestone pathways that led around the grass-covered grounds, turning to earthen byways as they twisted through part of the woods. There, various plants and flowers grew—some of them wild. Their bright colors dotted the land and added sweet fragrance to the air.

Regularly in the morning hours, the land looked foggy with a mist that gathered in the night. It was not so unusual an occurrence since they were close to Scotland. However, the mist only added to the servant's superstitious fears, and often they would warn about venturing out in it too late or too early. Isabel laughed at such warnings, shaking her head in tolerant bemusement.

Turning her steps toward the library where her father could usually be found, Isabel took a deep breath and patted her hair. As she reached for the door, it opened. To her dismay, she came face to chest with Colonel Wallace. Realizing there was no escaping the social necessity, she curtsied. Her gaze barely moved over his rigid face and, what Isabel believed to be, a persistently disapproving expression.

"Colonel Wallace," she acknowledged with a polite nod of her head. She refused to smile at him, not wanting to encourage any misplaced affection he might have developed for her.

"Miss Drake," he returned in his usual curt fashion. "I was hoping to meet with you this morning."

"Oh." Isabel looked away. With forced airiness, she claimed, "I cannot imagine what for."

"It is my wish to be allowed to call on you this evening, before supper, of course," said the Colonel. His tone was hard and matter-of-fact, leaving no room for doubts of his intentions.

He speaks to me as if I was one of his men to be ordered about, Isabel thought in disgust.

Flippantly, she responded, "Well, alas, good sir. It cannot be my wish. My afternoon is already promised to another. I believe you have been introduced to Mr. Tanner?" She waited for his reluctant nod. "I thought as much."

Before she could continue, the Colonel said, "Most unfortunate for me. Your parents, however, have invited me to dine tonight, and I should be happy to speak with you at that time. Good day, Miss Drake."

"Good day, Colonel," she answered with a curtsey to match his bow, unable to do otherwise after such an abrupt dismissal. She waited until he was out the front door before turning to join her father.

"Isabel!" the Viscountess, Lady Sutherfeld, exclaimed. Her mother graciously smiled, as she stood from her place in a low chair.

Isabel eyed her mother's good humor with a sense of

foreboding. Nodding, she acknowledged, "Mother. Father."

"Come in, Issie, come in," Lord Sutherfeld said with a merry wave, favoring his eldest daughter with a smile as he motioned for her to take a seat.

Isabel dutifully obeyed. Her father cleared his throat and then turned to some of the papers on his desk. Gathering them up, he organized and stacked them neatly into a pile.

Isabel waited as her father went through the ritual of looking busy as he collected his thoughts. Seeing a frown develop the more he collected, she fidgeted uneasily. Glancing at her mother's happy blue eyes, she learned nothing from the woman but that she was pleased with herself, as was always the case when her mother was concerned.

The Viscountess was a pretty woman for her advanced years. And though she was prone to a hearty dislike of her eldest child—whom she blamed for the slight roundness of her figure—she often hid it behind a smiling mask, knowing that many men had admired her for her dainty contrivances of pleasure.

When her father did not readily speak, she said, "The Colonel told me you asked him to dine this evening. I wish it were not so for I have already allowed

Mr. Tanner to come this afternoon. It was my hope that you would also see fit to allow him to dine."

"Well, of course, we would not want to appear inhospitable to your guest," said the Viscountess. She looked helplessly at her husband, clearly desiring him to deny his daughter's request. When he did not answer, her mother muttered, "But perhaps the invitation would be better if postponed to another night."

"I don't see why, Mother," Isabel protested as meekly as she could manage. "Colonel Wallace should not mind. Already, I have told him of Mr. Tanner coming today to see me—"

"Oh, Isabel," the Viscountess gasped. "You did no such thing!"

"Why, yes, Mother. I saw no reason not to. Besides, the Colonel is rather tiresome company, and I think that table conversation could be lightened by what Mr. Tanner has to impart." Her smile might have looked sweet, but inside she wanted to scream.

"I'm sorry to hear you say that," the Viscount stated before his wife could speak in an attempt to stop the fight brewing between the two women. Isabel watched her father expectantly. The Viscountess looked demurely at her lap. He continued, "We will get to the Colonel in a moment. First, I have to discuss something of great discontent to us all. Miss Martens."

Isabel cringed, having completely forgotten her latest disagreement with the governess. "Oh, Father, you cannot believe anything that dreadful woman says."

"That dreadful woman is the finest governess we could get to come—," her mother started.

The Viscount cleared his throat, interrupting his wife. "Miss Martens is a highly competent woman, and you vexed her quite grievously. She has left her position here as of this morning."

Good! Isabel thought. She hid her triumphant smile. It had taken her only two short months to get rid of the insufferable woman. "I wish I could say I was sorry for it, but the woman was a bore. And I daresay her French was that of...*lower society*."

The Viscountess paled at such a thought and was for once at a loss for words.

"Be that as it may, you need someone to guide you," her father said.

"I am above the age of needing a governess," Isabel complained, unable to hide her pout. "I have just turned twenty-one. I am not a child to be led about by the hand."

"That has yet to be proven," the Viscount muttered under his breath. Seeing his daughter's stricken face, he added, "I have decided not to get you another governess."

"That's wonderful," Isabel exclaimed happily.

"What?" the Viscountess said in horror. "My dear,

dear lord husband, you cannot mean for me to escort our daughters everywhere? Whenever would I have the time?"

"No, my lady." The Viscount's eyes held only a passing fondness for his wife as he looked at her. She was an amiable companion to him, one who had still been blessed with charm and looks even after children. For that, he gave small thanks. "I have decided that our daughters need someone more commanding to educate Jane properly and not be frightened away by Isabel's outspokenness."

"Father?" Isabel asked in growing apprehension.

"I will hire you a tutor." Her father was clearly proud of his own cleverness. "I think an educated man is just the thing for our Issie."

"But, propriety," the Viscountess argued, paling with the threat of a swoon. She frantically fanned her face.

"Get ahold of yourself, my lady." The Viscount was unaffected by his wife's theatrics. "Mr.—"

"Father?" Isabel whispered, not hearing him. "Tell me you are joking."

The Viscount continued as if she hadn't spoken. "He is beyond reproach. I have the highest recommendation of his character and have spoken extensively about him with the Colonel. Now, Colonel Wallace has allowed that such a fine character of sound mind and impeccable reputation will not be improper at all, considering Isabel is never alone with the man in private. And it is my hope that you, my dear Issie, will learn from him the proper discourse to be had with a gentleman. No more speaking of horseflesh and breeding, do you hear me?"

Isabel flinched. Miss Martens had caught her conversation with Mr. Tanner the week before and had harped endlessly. She should have known the woman would have tattled to her father about it.

"And why would the Colonel be involved in such a decision as to my tutor?" she inquired with a frown. Seeing her mother's teary smile, she felt her body weaken.

"Colonel Wallace is rather taken with your charms, my dear," her father answered.

"Yes, quite taken," echoed her mother with a nod of her head.

"What are you saying, Father? By all means, speak plainly." Isabel gripped the sides of the chair, her gloved hands working hard against the rough material. Her cheeks burned with the first simmer of anger.

"He wishes to marry you, daughter, and I have given him my consent. We have agreed that, after some intensive training of your mind and actions, he will claim you as his wife and formally introduce you to his uncle." The

Viscount appeared a bit puzzled by her reaction. "Surely, you know of his feelings?"

"No, I do not," Isabel answered.

"Isabel, your tone," her mother scolded.

"I will not mind my tone." She stood, desiring nothing more than to run away. "You must send him notice at once that you have changed your mind."

"I will do no such thing." Her father remained calm. "A gentleman does not rescind on his word without good cause. And you can forget Mr. Tanner. I will never consent to such a disagreeable man as he."

"But the *Colonel*? He wishes to change me," Isabel whispered in a mix of anger and mortification. "Am I not suited as I am? He would turn me into a meek and mild plaything?"

"You overreact." The Viscount scowled in displeasure. His tone became hard. "We merely wish to see your more desirable traits polished before you are to be a wife."

"Our family remaining in this home may very well be dependent on the impression you make upon his uncle," her mother inserted.

"And you will not be entertaining Mr. Tanner tonight or again unless it is with the Colonel's consent," her father said. "Mr. Tanner has been a most unwelcome influence over you, Issie."

"You *will* receive the Colonel's attentions tonight, daughter," her mother insisted.

"I will not," Isabel growled through clenched teeth. "If he wishes to speak to me, he will hear my thoughts. I will not have him. He will be wasting his time for the very character of my person, which he finds so objectionable, cannot and will not be changed. So I beg you, spare the Colonel the embarrassment of asking."

"Will not have him? He is worth nearly seven thousand a year." Her mother fluttered her hands nervously before her face, hovering between the desire to scold her daughter and the need to faint to prove how upset she was. "You could not hope to do much better. And as to change, a wife's place is nothing if not sacrifice."

"And, after his uncle passes, he will own Rothfield Park," put in her father logically. "He will be the new Marquis of Rothfield."

Isabel took several deep breaths. They were serious. They wanted her to give up her chance at happiness for a man with seven thousand a year and a house whose location she abhorred.

"If you don't marry him," her mother threatened, "I shall never speak to you again. And neither shall your father."

"Then I look forward to a long and happy silence," Isabel shouted. She rushed through the library door.

Seeing Jane's worried face as she passed through the front hall, Isabel met her sister's stricken expression and experienced a moment's regret. She refused to cry as she ran from the house as fast as she could.

Ignoring Jane's gentle entreaties, Isabel made her way quickly to the stables. The angry red of outrage and horror stung her porcelain features, burning violently against her skin.

Not seeing a groom to help her, she went to her mare. Grabbing a set of reins from the stall, she fashioned them about the horse's neck. Then, leading the palfrey out into the diffused sunlight, she brought the horse to the stairs so that she could maneuver onto its back with as much incensed grace as possible. Seated without the benefit of a sidesaddle, she nudged the mare and tore off toward the north field where the grass was the most open.

The spirited mare bolted forward with a jerk. Isabel, having ridden since the age of four, did not think twice about her wild ride. Her skirts flew behind her, pressing against her legs and fanning over the backside of the horse. When she was well into the field, she discovered she had two choices. Either she could ride out into the clearing, obviously within view of the library window, or she could ride into the mist, far from her father's watchful gaze.

Isabel chose the mist.

Once out of sight, she swung her leg over the mare's back and adjusted her skirts so that she was better seated astride the horse. The mist grew heavier, but she ignored it. She raced past shrubs and then trees. The mare found an easy path. Its hooves pounded down a gentle incline, through a limb covered alcove.

The fog thickened. Isabel reined the mare to a rough stop. She could hear the gentle babble of the nearby stream, but she could not see the water. The horse's hooves pattered nervously. The mist continued to expand and thicken until she could barely detect the trees in front of her.

She looked around in mounting terror. Her attention snapped to one side and then the other. The trees faded completely, leaving behind an all-consuming whiteness. The water grew louder until she could not tell from which direction it came. Maneuvering the horse around, she urged the palfrey to move. In the beginning, the animal resisted but finally obeyed as she yelled at it to go.

Isabel leaned close to the horse's neck, willing it to feel its way home. The fog only thickened. The horse's movements were slow and cautious. The animal's ears twitched, and its head bobbed in agitation.

Isabel forced a scared laugh, even as she trembled. The flesh on the back of her neck prickled in warning. She hugged closer to the skittish mare. She could feel its hot, sweaty flesh pressing into her gown. As they moved, she watched the white fog, willing her eyes to detect anything familiar. A tree limb passed close to her face. She jolted back in alarm.

And then she heard singing, the sweet chime of a child's voice in play. The melody was haunted and hard, despite its joyful laughter. It echoed in the trees. At first, it was behind her, running through the mist. However as she urged the horse faster, it was beside her, keeping pace with the mare.

"Play," she heard the childlike whisper near her ear.

Isabel jolted in fright. Tears slid over her cheeks. She bit her lip to keep from crying out. The singing came from her side, growing louder. The fog became so dense she could barely see the horse's ears pointed with alertness.

"Hello?" she called, her voice cracking. "Who's there?"

"Play," demanded the pouting voice.

"Who are you?" Isabel insisted. She couldn't see her hands. Her limbs shook. She was too afraid to move from the comfort of the horse's back. She felt the mare shake and jolt with each ring of laughter, each start of an eerie ballad. "What do you want?"

Suddenly, the laughing turned to tears. The mist seemed to press into Isabel's skin. She breathed it into her lungs like the smoke from a fire. Coughing, she wheezed to catch her breath. Almost instantly, perspiration dotted her flesh. The horse neighed and bucked in protest. Her fingers found her throat, tearing at her gown as she fought for air.

"I want to play with you," the child answered with a sulk in her voice. The sound of her words were hollow, garbled by a roaring Isabel couldn't make out. She coughed louder, desperate to get out of the fog. Sweetly, the voice asked, "Are you my mother? Are you the girl from my bedchamber?"

"No!" Isabel kicked her horse in the ribs, urging it forward, not caring if she was still within the trees. She would much rather take her chances against the forest.

As the startled mare began to gallop, a hand shot out from the fog trying to stop her. The masculine fingers reached for the horse's reins. It was the hand of a man—pale, strained, and strong. She saw the ruffling of a shirt. Isabel screamed louder. Her mare jolted violently, and she lost the reins. The hand disappeared behind her. She sat up, looking over her shoulder to see if the man was coming for her. There was nothing but mist all around.

With a relieved sigh, she turned to look forward. Her eyes did not have time to focus as a branch materialized out of the fog. It struck her across the forehead, knocking her back with a sharp crack. Blood filled her mouth. Her head hit the jolting movements of the animal's galloping rump. Her feet loosened their hold, and she flipped over the back of the horse to the ground. And, as her head struck the earth, the white mist turned into enveloping darkness.

To find out more about Michelle's books visit www.MichellePillow.com

www.ingramcontent.com/pod-product-compliance
Lightning Source LLC
Chambersburg PA
CBHW050255110726
47898CB00007B/2414